Dear Reader

Have you ever thought about a dream job? For me it was being a flight attendant for an international airline back in the day. I travelled the world—at the airline's expense—I saw exotic locales I could never afford to visit on my own. And I met the most wonderful and incredible people along the way.

Not everyone is so lucky as to get to travel like that. Other jobs provide other ways. Come join Stacey Williams as she lives her dream as a Vacation Nanny—travelling to foreign countries, seeing sights she'd never be able to afford to on her own, combining her love for children with her desire to see the world. She has it all.

Yet after years of this dream job she's wondering if there might be something more. What does the future hold? A family, perhaps? Can she find the right man to build a future with? Who can replace the excitement of travel with love and devotion and a world for two that will be so special she'd never miss her job?

How does a nanny meet an eligible bachelor? And, if she meets him, how can she surmount the obstacles he erects every step of the way?

I hope you enjoy Stacey's journey. The setting is near Altea, on the Costa Blanca, where my parents lived for many years. I have such lovely memories of spending an entire summer in Spain. I hope to go back one day. But in the meantime—I'm enjoying it through Stacey's eyes.

All the best

Barbara

THE NANNY
AND THE
BOSS'S TWINS

BY
BARBARA McMAHON

First published in Great Britain 2012
by Mills & Boon, an imprint of Harlequin (UK) Limited.
Harlequin (UK) Limited, Eton House, 18-24 Paradise Road,
Richmond, Surrey TW9 1SR

© Barbara McMahon 2012

ISBN: 978 (

Harlequin (U
and recyclabl
forests. The l
legal environ

Printed and bound in Great Britain
by CPI Antony Rowe, Chippenham, Wiltshire

Barbara McMahon was born and raised in the south USA, but settled in California after spending a year flying around the world for an international airline. After settling down to raise a family and work for a computer firm, she began writing when her children started school. Now, feeling fortunate in being able to realise her long-held dream of quitting her 'day job' and writing full time, she and her husband have moved to the Sierra Nevada mountains of California, where she finds her desire to write is stronger than ever. With the beauty of the mountains visible from her windows, and the pace of life slower than the hectic San Francisco Bay Area where they previously resided, she finds more time than ever to think up stories and characters and share them with others through writing. Barbara loves to hear from readers. You can reach her at PO Box 977, Pioneer, CA 95666-0977, USA. Readers can also contact Barbara at her website: www.barbaramcmahon.com

Other books by Barbara McMahon:

ANGEL OF SMOKY HOLLOW
FIREFIGHTER'S DOORSTEP BABY
MARRYING THE SCARRED SHEIKH

To my wonderful editor, Lucy Gilmour, for being such a gem to work with and always uplifting her authors. Thank you, Lucy!

CHAPTER ONE

STACEY WILLIAMS checked her watch for the tenth time. It was still a few minutes before the agreed-upon time, but still she scanned the crowd as passengers walked by. The international terminal at Kennedy Airport was crowded as people checked in for flights all over the world. She had the correct check-in line, she'd verified that before she'd begun her vigil, but she didn't have a ticket. Her new boss would have her ticket.

Watching for Luis Aldivista, she zeroed in on any men with children in attendance. She'd recognize the twin boys and their father after meeting with them yesterday. Still, she scanned each face. Would their regular nanny accompany them to the airport? Or was Luis arriving here expecting her to take charge immediately? Their meeting yesterday had been necessarily brief. Only after she'd left had she thought of questions.

There, a tall dark-haired man with two children—and a woman carrying a baby right beside him. For a moment Stacey felt a pang of envy. She and her sister were all the family each had, but one day she'd love to fall in love, get married and have a family of her own with lots of children. She loved children—it was why she did the job she did, but watching other people's children wasn't the same as raising some of her own.

She was jostled as the crowd grew. It was prime time for late afternoon departures and more and more people arrived by the moment. JFK International Airport was one of the country's busiest, and with the start of summer vacations she expected it would continue to be crowded for the next several weeks.

She checked her watch again and, looking up, she spotted the man holding two squirmy boys enter the terminal. A porter pushed a luggage cart behind them. It struck her again that Luis didn't fit her idea of a typical Spaniard. Instead of the dark hair she'd expected, this man had sandy brown hair. He was tall, and fit, but the strong jaw and tightly pressed lips also didn't fit her image of a fiery Latino. Somehow in the past she'd always pictured Spanish men as lovers, with soft words to whisper into a woman's ear and a delightful manner in making a woman feel special.

Luis looked nothing like her fantasies.

He looked around the terminal, spotted her and said something to the boys. They both looked up at him at the same time. She smiled at the twin expressions. When she'd met them yesterday she'd wondered how she'd ever tell them apart. They were identical in every way—except personality. Juan was much more outgoing than his brother Pablo.

She pulled her bag behind her as she approached them, her travel tote slung over one shoulder.

"Mr. Aldivista," she greeted him as she got closer.

He looked at her. "Right on time, I see."

She nodded and looked at the boys, smiling. Both clung to their father and studied her with wary eyes.

"Boys, say hello to Miss Williams."

"I don't want to go," one of the boys complained.

"I don't need a babysitter," the other protested, frown-

ing at Stacey. His look mirrored that of his father. She knew they would be a handful. She'd seen evidence of that on their pre-trip interview yesterday, but she was up to the challenge. She hoped.

When she'd showed up for the interview, Luis Aldivista's first comment had been about her appearance—too young to be a nanny for his boys. Even a temporary nanny for their trip to Spain. For a second she'd thought he'd refuse to hire her but, having left it so close to their departure date, there wasn't a lot he could do.

She'd explained again the credentials of all the nannies in the company. She herself had graduated from college with a degree in early childhood education, and then taken the course from the prestigious Miss Pritchards' School for Nannies. Which he already knew since Stephanie, their office manager, had provided references and credentials when he had visited the agency.

She should be used to people thinking she looked too young for the job, she heard it often enough. One of her friends had said she'd appreciate that youthful look when she was much older and the rest of their peer group looked like dried apples, but she wasn't there yet and it grew annoying.

Luis's lips tightened even more. "Stop that behavior," he told his boys. He glanced at Stacey. "I hope this trip isn't going to be a mistake. We're not even on the plane and they're already causing problems."

"Then let me take charge, that's what you hired me for," she said brightly, feeling the tension rise. She'd arrived home yesterday from another assignment and had scarcely had time to make the interview. Normally she liked to spend a bit more time with the children she'd be watching than just a brief ten-minute meeting, but Stacey was one of only two nannies in their agency who spoke

Spanish. There wasn't much choice in the matter if she was to uphold the reputation of Vacation Nannies. Luis Aldivista wasn't the only one wondering if the trip was going to prove a mistake.

"Tell me your names again, please," she said to the twins.

"I'm Juan," the boy on the left said. Pointing to his twin, he continued, "He's Pablo."

"Are you looking forward to the plane ride?" she asked.

"I don't want to go."

"I don't want you here. I want Hannah," Juan said with a pout, then looked up at his father.

"Hannah isn't coming. We've been over this a hundred times. Stacey will be your temporary nanny while we are on vacation," Luis said with little patience. "Let's get going. The sooner we get through security, the sooner we'll be on our way."

Signaling the porter to follow, he led the way to the line for first-class check-in. Moments later all bags except his laptop and her tote had been whisked away.

Stacey didn't have much chance to talk with the boys with everything going on and she determined that while they waited at the departure gate she'd try to learn more about them and have them get to know her better. From the brief interview, she knew they could be a handful. But with their regular nanny at their side, they'd had a modicum of courtesy. Now they were just obstreperous boys uncertain about the changes ahead.

Vacation Nannies had been her idea. She and her sister had founded the small boutique agency five years ago. The idea was to match qualified nannies with families needing childcare for limited periods of time—usually when on vacation. Savannah had still been in college

when they'd come up with the concept and had immediately added some business courses to help with starting the firm. After only a year in operation, they'd realized they had a goldmine and had expanded to include other qualified nannies. Two years later they had rented their current office space and hired Stephanie to coordinate everything. They now had a dozen nannies. Their reputation was sterling and they were daily getting more requests than they could handle.

She kept an eye on the boys, though they still held onto their father's hands. They were not charming sweet children like those of her last assignment. They complained. They contradicted each other with constant bickering, and they tugged constantly on their father's hand, as if trying to break away.

Once through security, Luis stopped out of the stream of passengers and looked at her. "I need to make a phone call to the office. Take charge, please, and I'll meet you all at the gate before we board."

Nothing like being dumped into the deep end of an assignment, she thought, nodding, reaching for the boys' hands. She was not going to let them roam free. She had a sudden vision of them running in two different directions and her trying to find them.

"I don't want to go with you," Juan said. Or was it Pablo? No, it was Juan. She needed a way to tell them apart.

"Your dad'll meet us before we get on the plane. Come along, let's find our gate."

"I don't want to go to Spain," Pablo said.

"I've never been. Have you?" she asked, trying to defuse the loaded statement.

He shook his head. "I want Hannah."

"Hannah's taking a short vacation herself," Stacey

explained. The boys' regular nanny had refused to accompany them to Spain. Her excuse was a fear of flying, but Stacey was beginning to wonder if it was just to have a few weeks to herself after dealing with them all the time.

"She's our nanny, you're not."

"I want to go with her on vacation." Juan said.

"You're going to see your great-grandmother. Hannah's going to visit her family. I'll be flying with you and watch you while on vacation."

They both pouted and Stacey had to look away lest they see her smile. Twins were adorable as a rule and these two would probably prove the same once she got to know them better. If their manners improved a bit. If they got over not wanting to go.

She found their gate and sat down with the boys on either side to await their father's return. Despite his hesitancy yesterday, he'd had no trouble immediately giving her charge of his children. Wasn't he the slightest bit concerned how they'd all get along? Or was he the stereotypical workaholic, too caught up in the challenges of business to really pay attention to his sons?

Luis Aldivista listened as his head of sales brought him up to speed on the negotiations they were in the midst of. Several years ago he'd invented medical software that interfaced directly between doctors' offices and their affiliated hospitals. Gradually they'd begun selling to the east coast and into the midwest but now they were poised to expand into the western part of the country and Luis wanted to stay on top of things.

This was important. He wished he could have convinced his grandmother of that. But the invitation had been a nicely worded summons. Since he owed his

grandmother a lot, he couldn't refuse. It would be the first time she'd asked him to return to Spain since the boys' birth, although she'd visited several times, so she knew the twins. But they'd never been to the place he would forever think of as home.

Still, the timing sucked.

When he finished talking with Jerry, he had his secretary transfer him to his research and development team so he could get an update on the latest version of the software, due to be released in six weeks. Luis wanted daily updates.

He'd only left the office four hours ago. He checked his watch. Their flight would be departing soon and by the time they landed, New York would be fast asleep. This was his last chance to be in touch with the office for a while.

Once he'd hung up, he swung by a coffee kiosk and got a cup of coffee. He had work to do on the plane, and with the flight time such as it was, his circadian rhythm would be all messed up by the time he landed in Spain.

As he approached the waiting area for the flight, he quickly located his new temporary nanny and his sons. She was talking to them and for once the boys seemed to be behaving. They both sat in seats, watching her as she talked. At least they hadn't dashed off, trying to find him. Or trying to get home. He would have thought they'd love the opportunity to take a trip to Spain. If only his long-term nanny had accompanied them.

Stacey spotted him and smiled. He nodded in acknowledgment. He had to give her points for already controlling those hellion boys of his. He wished he knew her secret. Even Hannah had trouble with them, but for once it seemed they were not getting into mischief.

"Everything okay at your office?" she asked.

He shrugged. "This is not the best time to be taking a vacation. I'm needed here."

Although he was taking both his phone and his laptop and expected to work from his grandmother's home, making this very much a working holiday.

"But what a great opportunity for you and the boys. I think traveling is so educational," she said.

"They're a little young to be viewing the trip as educational. It would have suited me more to wait a few years."

Luis knew the company would be in good hands while he was gone. He paid high wages to keep the best in the business. His general manager was more than competent in running things. Still, it felt odd to be taking off at such a crucial time—and for three weeks. He hadn't taken a real vacation since selling that first version of the software to the doctors' consortium in Boston. It was actually pushing six years.

"Go now and again in a few years as well," she said with a smile.

Stacey turned her attention to Juan, who was complaining again. Luis knew his sons—they'd get worse and worse until he'd have to send them to their rooms. Impossible now they were about to board a plane! He hoped they slept through the flight. How did other parents have perfectly behaved children when his acted like hellions most of the time?

He took the seat on the far side of Pablo, glad the nanny had saved it for him. Stacey continued to talk to them about airplanes and the boys seemed enthralled. He still thought the woman looked little older than a teenager, but so far she'd shown she had a knack with kids. He couldn't remember the last time the twins had sat so still or been so attentive.

Maybe they just like looking at her? He had to admit, she was pretty.

He frowned. Her long blonde hair was pulled back into a low ponytail. Her bright blue eyes drew his attention again and again. She had a light tan but, if he had to describe her, he would call her complexion peaches and cream.

Looking away, he checked his watch again. He wasn't interested in his nanny as a person, only as someone who would take care of his children. They'd begin boarding soon, and he had more important things to concentrate on than how pretty the temporary nanny was, though she definitely spiked his interest. It had been a long time since he'd had any interest in the opposite sex. But this was not a complication he wanted. He was confusing awareness with gratitude. That was it. He was grateful she had taken Hannah's place on such short notice, they couldn't have made the trip otherwise. He didn't want to take the boys to his grandmother's without someone to watch them. He'd be too busy himself. And there was no guarantee a nanny in Spain would speak English.

Stacey glanced at Luis, noting the frown. Did he never smile? The boys wanted to go to the large windows to look at planes, so she took each by the hand and soon all three were watching planes take off and absorbing the size of the one they'd be on, which was already parked at the gate.

She recalled what Stephanie had told her just before she'd set out for the Aldivista residence to interview and be interviewed. Luis Aldivista had been on New York's top ten most eligible bachelors list the last couple of years. He'd invented some kind of medical software that most of the private doctors' offices in the country used.

Stephanie hadn't dealt with details. All that had been important to her was that his software had made him fabulously wealthy. But Luis was so good looking he might have made the list without the money behind him.

Stacey wasn't sure of her friend's assessment. So far the man looked grumpy. And so focused on business he couldn't share his children's delight with airplanes. He needed to lighten up if they were all to enjoy this trip.

"What's that one, Stacey?" one of the twins asked.

Stacey stooped down to be at eye level with the little boy. He was adorable—blond curls that went every which way, bright blue eyes that seem to sparkle from inside. "That's called a jumbo jet. Because it's a jumbo size. I'm not sure who makes it. We can look that up when we get to Spain if you like."

She looked at their father. He was totally involved in whomever he was talking to on the phone. She wanted to snatch it away and tell him to enjoy the excitement of a first flight with his sons. He should be the one explaining how planes flew and where in the world they could all be going. But she was used to fathers who put work ahead of children. They did what they did. A mere nanny wasn't going to change that.

Turning back to the planes, she wondered why men married and had families if they didn't want to spend time with them. If she ever got married and had her family, she'd insist her husband spend time with her and their children.

If ever. She sighed. Her job didn't give her much chance to meet eligible bachelors.

She looked at the boys. The twins must take after their mother. Luis had brown hair and hazel eyes. Not that she should be noticing that.

"Cute children you have." A woman had brought her

daughter to the window to look out. "They look just like you. Their first plane ride?"

Stacey was taken aback by the comment, but then smiled and responded with, "Yes. We're flying to Spain." No need to say more, she'd never see the woman again.

"Ah, have a great time. We're on our way to Italy. My husband's there on business and we're joining him for a short vacation."

Juan looked up at Stacey and tugged on her hand. "When do we get to go inside the plane?" he asked. "I want to see inside the plane," he went on, pressing his face against the glass.

"You'll see it from the inside once we get on board. Look, there's one taking off," she said, pointing. They watched the planes for a minute, then Stacey felt Pablo tugging on her shirt.

"I want to see inside, too," he said.

"We will, sweetie. Just be patient. Look at that big one coming in to land. I wonder where it's flying in from?"

"Maybe Spain," Juan said.

"Maybe Ohio," Pablo said.

"Ohio?" Stacey was surprised he knew about other states.

"Hannah's going on vacation to Ohio. I miss her."

Stacey stooped down and hugged him. "Of course you do. And I know she misses you. So we'll write her a letter when we get to Spain. You can keep a journal of all your adventures to share with her when you return home."

"What's a journal?" Juan asked. "Can I keep one too?"

"A journal is writing down what happens each day to help you remember."

"I can write my name," Juan said proudly.

"I'll help with the writing, you two can tell me what to write and then Hannah can read it when you get home."

"Can we write about the big planes?" Pablo asked.

"Sure, that would be a great start. We'll get a notebook as soon as we get to your grandmother's. And I have my camera with me. We'll take pictures so you can remember." She pulled out a digital camera and snapped a few shots of the planes they could see, and also took a couple of the boys in the busy terminal. She loved keeping journals of the trips, both for herself and the children she watched.

"I can't wait to go on the plane," Juan said.

Before she could say more the first boarding announcement sounded and she smiled at him. "We get to get on it now."

She nodded at to the other woman. "Have a good flight."

The boys ran back toward their father, pulling on her hands. "We get to go inside the plane now, Daddy!"

"So I heard," Luis said, rising. Laptop in hand, he motioned to them to precede him and in only moments they were inside the first-class cabin.

"Daddy, that other lady said we look like Stacey. We don't, we look like us," one of the twins said, bouncing up and down on his seat.

Luis looked at her questioningly.

"I think she thought they were mine. Blond hair, blue eyes. Not much of a resemblance beyond that."

"Melissa, their mom, had blonde hair, darker than yours, more like honey. Her eyes were light blue."

They had the four seats in one row, two each side of the aisle. "I'll sit by one of the boys for part of the trip and you the other. We can switch halfway through," Luis

suggested as they matched boarding passes to seat assignments.

"Perfect," she said. That'd give her time to visit with the each boy individually and learn more about them.

Juan sat next to her in the window seat. Pablo sat in the window seat next to his father. Stacey knew that Pablo was shy around strangers, though she hoped he'd warm up to her quickly. They'd be together a lot over the next three weeks.

As the jumbo jet made a smooth take-off, Luis leaned back in his seat and looked across the aisle at the new nanny. She was bent close to Juan, listening as his son regaled her with some tale. For a moment he wished he could capture the sight in a photograph. His boys were special. He wished they'd forever be as happy as Juan looked right now. He didn't often see that expression.

It was at special moments like this he missed Melissa with an ache that seemed destined to never fade. She had missed every moment of their lives, dying of an aneurism before delivering Pablo. She'd never even held her sons. At every milestone, he offered up the hope that Melissa knew, somewhere, somehow.

Stacey enjoyed sitting by Juan, happy he was so easy to travel with. He talked her ear off non-stop from the time the doors closed until the flight was airborne. He'd loved looking out the window until land was left behind. He thought the ocean was boring. Once or twice she glanced over at Luis and Pablo. That twin was quieter. He seemed intent on coloring in pages his father produced from the packet Hannah had sent. Her own contributions to keep the children entertained had yet to be opened. Hannah had packed small toys they could play with in the confined space of their seats.

Luis settled Pablo then opened his laptop and seemed

totally engrossed with whatever he was reading, his expression thoughtful, his eyes focused on the screen. His hair was a bit mussed. Had he run his fingers through when she'd not been looking?

And why was she looking? She was here for the children, not to watch the father. Had it been just over twenty-four hours ago that she had met him for the first time? She'd returned to her office after meeting the boys and studied the interview sheets with more intensity than normal. He was widowed. He was head of a very successful software development firm. And he was so good looking he should carry a warning label.

When she'd gone home, she'd looked him up on the internet, and found the article Stephanie had mentioned that listed him as one of New York's most eligible bachelors. No mention of his kids. Several tremendous photographs, however, would have everyone in New York recognizing him if they met him on the street.

She turned back to Juan. How lucky Luis was to have his twins. She hoped they were making family memories for the boys to cherish in the future. She only had vague memories of her own mother and father. She'd been six when delivered to Grams, her sister Savannah only four. And her mother's mother had been arthritic and grumpy and already in her mid-sixties. If Stacey hadn't had her sister, she didn't know what she would have done. Savannah and she had made the most of whatever Grams had offered, but they hadn't had much materially or done much outside the home. No travel, no vacations. When she'd turned eighteen, she'd deliberately set out to change her future for the better.

Stretching slightly, she acknowledged her own good luck to spend the next three weeks at some Spanish villa by the sea. When growing up in Palmerville, West

Virginia, she'd dreamed about the sea. Now her best assignments were the ones at the beach. Thankfully the rich and famous liked the beach as much as she did.

During the meal service, she assisted Juan in cutting his meat and helping with his beverage. Once the meal service ended, she asked if Luis wanted to switch boys. Juan protested about going to sit by his dad, he wanted to stay with Stacey. Since the seats were large, she agreed and Pablo joined them. Soon the three of them were engrossed in putting together a puzzle she'd brought. The boys had never done a jigsaw puzzle before and vied with each other to match pieces to the spaces, often trying to force them in until Stacey explained they needed to reconstruct the picture and pieces in wrong places simply would not do!

She glanced again at her new employer. He was still working on the laptop, but she knew the battery would be dying soon. Then what would he do?

Her years working in this job had convinced her business tycoons didn't have a family gene. They might want a family, but it was mainly for show or to leave the family fortune to. Children were nice to have brought out to meet associates and then shunted off in the care of someone else.

Her grandmother had been sickly, but she'd done her best for Stacey and her sister. She'd read to them, and taught them how to keep house, cook, mend clothes. All of it accompanied with family stories about relatives who had died without Stacey ever meeting them. Still, those were her family memories of growing up. Poor, deprived of bicycles and other toys her schoolmates had enjoyed, she still had those cherished memories. She missed her grandmother.

Growing up poor, however, had fostered the desire

to enjoy luxury, hence the idea of being a temporary nanny, where she got to travel to exotic locations. While not participating in the activities of the parents, the children still had wonderful amenities that she would have loved as a child and she did her best to give each child a wonderful memory of the vacation, whether spending time with their parents or not.

She wondered about her current boss. He'd mentioned spending summers in Spain. With his parents? Or had he been shuffled off to get out of the way for their own lifestyles? She doubted she'd ever find out. Curiosity had her wondering about him while his children played quietly. Soon she'd try to get them to sleep a bit. It was already dark outside. They'd be landing in Madrid early in the morning. Sleep was required!

Midway through the flight the boys gave up and she reclined the seat they shared, covered them with a blanket and gave them each a pillow. In only seconds they were both fast asleep.

Which gave Stacey plenty of time to think. Her eyes were drawn to Luis Aldivista. His concentration seemed complete, which enabled her to study him without him being aware of it. He was better looking than the photographs she'd seen on the internet. What were his expectations for the trip?

"Mr. Aldivista," she said softly. The jet was so quiet she knew he could hear her and she didn't want to wake the boys.

He looked over. "Yes?" It took him a moment to focus. What was he thinking? she wondered.

"I thought maybe we should talk a bit more about what you expect from the trip. Will I be taking the boys around sightseeing, or will we be primarily at your grandmother's place?"

"At Abuela Maria's, I imagine," he said, frowning slightly. "I don't have any expectations. Just watch them. Keep them out of mischief. Try to have them behave."

"Why wouldn't they?" she asked, wondering if there was more to this assignment than she knew about.

"They're a handful. If one wants to do one thing, the other wants to do the opposite." He shook his head. "Hannah limits what they do because they're so much trouble."

Stacey glanced at the sleeping boys. They looked angelic to her.

"I think I can manage," she replied dryly. How hard could they be?

"See that you do. I don't want them disrupting my grandmother's home."

"I've never been to Spain, neither have they. I hope we see some of it while here. I'm sure the boys would love to see some of the old forts or castles."

He looked at his computer, sighed and closed it. "Battery's dead," he said. Then he looked back at Stacey. "My grandmother's home is right on the sea. The boys will find enough to do, playing on the beach. Easier to keep them corralled that way."

She tilted her head slightly. "Will you be spending much time with them?"

"No promises. I'll have to see how thing go at work."

She wanted him to say he'd already planned on spending time with Juan and Pablo every day, but she was tilting at windmills. Die-hard business tycoons like Luis Aldivista never put anything before business.

"They don't speak Spanish, do they?"

He shook his head.

"But you do?"

"Of course. I spent every summer in Spain from the

time I was younger than the boys until I went to college and had to work summers."

"Don't you think they'll have an easier time if you were with them some part of the day?"

"That's why I hired you, Ms. Williams. Are you not up to the task? If so, I wished you'd spoken up before we left New York."

"I'm more than capable of taking care of your children. I just thought—"

"I don't pay you to think. Please just do the job for which you were hired."

Stacey nodded, her enthusiasm dimming slightly. She gave him a polite smile when what she really wanted to do was bop him on the head. Turning away, she studied the sleeping boys for a moment. They looked angelic. And while their spirits had been high at the airport, she didn't sense any malice or mischief in either.

Knowing they would land very early in the morning in Madrid, she leaned back and tried to sleep. She'd made transatlantic crossings before, and knew the first day or so in Europe was tiring due to the time change and lack of sleep. Not that these little guys would have that. They'd be wired with excitement. She'd better catch some sleep while she could.

Before drifting to sleep, Stacey imagined Luis having a change of heart and wanting to spend time with his sons. Thinking back over all the families she'd worked for over the years, only one or two came to mind who actually put their children and family fun above all else on a vacation. She really wished that would change.

When they landed in Madrid, the boys were cranky. That set the mood for the next stage of the journey. The connection to their next flight was tight and going through

customs wasn't as fast as Stacey wished. Still, they made the next plane and were soon airborne again on the one-hour flight to the coast. Once they landed in Alicante, Luis had Stacey watch the boys while he went to get their luggage and pick up the rental car he'd had reserved.

Tired from their flight, a bit scared with all the commotion at the foreign airport and not understanding the language around them, the boys clung to Stacey and said they wanted to go home. She explained everything around them, and then asked about their great-grandmother, trying to divert them from focusing on what they didn't like.

"Have you ever met her?" she asked.

"She came to visit when we were little," Juan said.

She smiled. To her these boys were still little.

"She always smelled nice," Pablo added.

"So visiting her at her house will be fun, right?" she asked cheerfully.

"I want to go home," Pablo said yet again.

"You'll have fun this vacation, we'll make sure of that. Then when you go home you can tell Hannah all about your trip!" she said, trying to keep him from dwelling on his wish to return home.

Once in the rental car, Stacey sat in the front beside Luis and the boys sat together in the back.

"It's still about an hour's drive," Luis said, pulling out of the airport and getting on the highway. The traffic was heavy as people made their way to work. Soon, however, Alicante was left behind them as the car headed north.

Stacey gazed out the window as he drove. She saw glimpses of the sea from time to time. Anticipation rose. She hoped the weather would be good for the children's sake. It was so much easier to play by the water than in-

side a strange place in inclement weather. She was prepared for either eventuality, however.

Luis drove on autopilot. He was tired, not having slept
long on the plane. But as soon as he could get an internet connection, he'd send the office the work he'd done
and then catch a nap.

He glanced at Stacey. She was restful to be around and
didn't talk needlessly. Didn't flirt, didn't try to charm
him. He frowned. Where had that thought come from?
He was immune to women who were looking for a relationship, as his sister often said. Maybe he was, but he'd
been in love with Melissa and when she'd died, a part of
him had died as well.

Besides, if he ever did become interested in another
woman, it wouldn't be someone like Stacey Williams.
Melissa had been tall, blonde, a bit reserved and definitely sophisticated. While the coloring wasn't too different, Stacey was totally the opposite of Melissa.

Sophisticated wasn't the word he'd use for her. She
bubbled with life. Everything seemed like an adventure.
Though she had connected instantly with his sons.

His wife had been a real asset when he'd been courting
investors for the new firm he was starting. She'd known
how to entertain all levels of society. She'd always had
the right word, the right clothes. Not that he was thinking about marriage or a new wife. He'd had his shot. Now
he had his company—and his boys.

Still, Stacey was young, carefree and fun—just what
his sons needed. He looked at her again. She turned and
met his gaze, her eyes alight with delight.

"It's beautiful along here. I can't wait to see where
we'll be staying."

"The villa's larger than most. My grandmother had

six children. My father is third from the oldest. There's a guest cottage that sleeps ten as well. Plenty of room for all."

He wondered where his grandmother would put them. Would *she* get servant quarters? He hadn't thought about that. He hoped she wouldn't get all upset if that was the case.

He drove through the small village of Alta Parisa, the place he'd known so well from his childhood visits. They were almost at his grandmother's. Soon he turned into the familiar drive, curving around until the villa came into view. He was surprised by the feeling of homecoming. He'd spent many summers here with his sister while his parents had been off doing their own thing and he'd wondered as a teenager why they'd had two children if they didn't want to spend time with them.

The villa was surrounded by flowering plants. Purple bougainvillea trailed from the upper balcony down the columns surrounding the ground-level veranda. Gardenias scented the air with their sweet fragrance. Dahlias and zinnias and roses were artfully arranged to offer contrasting colors and textures against the cream color of the walls.

The tall windows on each floor were flanked by dark shutters that were rarely closed. The stucco gleamed in the sunshine. Beyond he saw the guest cottage a short walk from the main house through the gardens. To his right was the sea.

The boys were straining to see everything, curiosity finally erasing crankiness and homesickness. They'd be ready for a nap in the early afternoon, but Luis hoped they'd greet his grandmother without any attitude.

"We're here," Luis said needlessly. He glanced at his new nanny, wondering what she thought of the place.

Melissa had only come once and had been out of her element not speaking the language and not knowing anyone. That had been the only time she hadn't fit in perfectly, whatever the circumstances.

How would Stacey fare? Not that it mattered that much, she was only a temporary nanny after all. She'd be perfect for the boys, which would leave him free to spend time with his grandmother, cousins, and parents when they arrived. And to work.

"It's lovely," she said, still taking in everything.

He looked at the villa again, remembering racing around the upper balcony, chasing Isabella. They were only two years apart and except when the cousins had come to visit had had only themselves to play with those summers. There'd been no other children living close by. They'd had the run of the place and known every nook and cranny.

He hoped his sons would have happy memories of this visit. He glanced again at Stacey. She'd proved competent on the trip, keeping the boys entertained and under control. She'd been especially helpful at the airport in Madrid. She looked as fresh as she had when he'd first seen her at JFK. She turned to look at him and he was struck anew by how blue her eyes were. He stared a moment, time suspended. He could feel his interest intensify. If he let himself forget for a second she was in his employ, that she was there for his kids, would he do something foolish?

"Welcome to my grandmother's home," he said in Spanish.

"Thank you. I can't wait to see everything," she replied in the same language.

"I'll be happy to show you around. Come meet my grandmother." A cordial offer. He would make sure she

was satisfied without giving in to the need he suddenly felt to learn more about her. To get to know her. She was beautiful, no doubt, but he'd seen beautiful women before.

Stacey helped get the boys from the car and the four of them went to the huge double front doors, carved of dark wood, gleaming with a rich, dark finish. Knocking brought a maid in no time, who obviously knew Luis as she broke into rapid Spanish words of welcome. Hugging him, she looked at Stacey and the boys. Quickly she spoke again.

"Sorry, Camilla, they don't speak Spanish yet. Juan and Pablo, this is Camilla, she works for your great-grandmother and can always find a snack for a hungry boy," Luis said with a grin.

She beamed at the boys and spoke again.

"She says come visit with her when you get settled," Stacey translated.

The maid looked at her. "You speak Spanish," she said in that language.

"*Sí*. I'm Stacey, nanny to the boys. Perhaps you can show me where I should go?"

"Oh, *la señora* wishes to see all of you as soon as you arrive. Come in. What am I doing, talking when she awaits? Come, come. She's on the terrace by the sea. It's warm this morning, she's enjoying her chocolate there. Come, come."

Following her as she walked quickly through the villa, they soon came to a lovely terrace that was surrounded by flowers and straight ahead a view of the Med. The sea sparkled in the sunshine, reflecting the light like diamonds on the waves. The blue of the water was deeper than that of the clear sky.

An elderly woman sat at a table with another, enjoying their hot beverages.

"Ah, Luis, you have arrived!" The older of the two jumped up and rushed to greet him. She was dressed in black, her silvery hair fashioned in a short style suited to an active life.

Stacey watched as the petite woman embraced her much taller grandson, tears of happiness in her eyes. She then looked at the boys and hugged each of them, exclaiming on how big they'd gotten, how happy she was to have them visit, how she'd missed them. When she got to Stacey she smiled. "I'm Marie Aldivista. Welcome to my home."

"Stacey Williams, nanny for the boys," Stacey replied.

She frowned and looked at Luis. "I thought their nanny was older."

"Stacey is a vacation nanny only. Hannah's the boys' regular nanny and she is older, but she couldn't accompany us. Stacey's just for the trip." He spoke in Spanish.

Maria Aldivista looked at her again and smiled, a hint of speculation in her eyes. "So, welcome to España and to my house. May I call you Stacey?" She also spoke in her native tongue.

"I wish you would. I'm so pleased I could come to watch the boys. What I've seen so far is lovely. I can't wait to see more of the gardens and the beach."

"You must have spent time in Spain, your Spanish is excellent."

"I had a great teacher, but this is my first time in Spain," Stacey said, pleased with the compliment.

Maria looked at Luis. "You must show her the village and take her and the boys to some of the sights. This is the best part of Spain."

"So says a woman who has lived here all her life," he said with a smile of affection.

"So I should know, right? Come, sit. Have something to eat or drink. Sophia, welcome Luis and his boys and Stacey. You are all the first to arrive after my dear cousin."

Introductions were made to Sophia who, as far as Stacey could determine, was a distant cousin to Maria. They'd been girls together and Sophia had come for the birthday celebration. She remarked to Luis that his sons reminded her of him when he was young and came to visit his *abuela*.

Hot chocolate and fresh coffee were soon served and Luis's grandmother asked him about his work, the trip over and what he wanted to do while visiting.

Stacey listened, keeping an eye on the boys. They were growing bored and she thought it best if they went to their rooms, changed clothes and maybe took a short nap.

"Ah, the boys are growing restless," Maria said a moment later. She smiled at them. "Luis, show them the room you had as a boy. I've put you on the second floor in the room you used when you brought Melissa. I thought they'd be more comfortable on the third floor next to the playroom."

"You've kept the playroom?" he asked.

"Of course. Each generation has children. I want them all to love coming here as much as you did." She looked at Sophia. "I think I'll put Stacey in the rose room, what do you think?"

"She would do well there," Sophia said with a nod.

"Wherever you wish," Stacey said. "Is that next to the boys' room."

"No, it's on the floor below. There will be other chil-

dren on the third floor. The twins won't feel lonely. Luis, your cousins Sebastian and Theresa will be here tomorrow afternoon with their families. And the day after Miguel and Pedro and their families. I love it when the house is full of children. I'm sorry Isabella can't come until next week."

Luis looked thoughtfully at his grandmother. "And where is this rose room?" His grandmother looked at him. "It's on the second floor—right next to yours."

CHAPTER TWO

Luis kept his composure but he was not pleased with the obvious ploy on his grandmother's part. He knew she fervently believed men should have a wife to help in life's journey. She'd been very happy with his grandfather and wanted all her grandchildren married and as happy.

His sister Isabella and his cousin Sabrina were the only other unmarried members of the family. Did grandmother have plans for them as well?

He looked at Stacey. She glanced at him, a hint of amusement in her eyes. She'd definitely picked up on his grandmother's machinations. Would it give her ideas? He didn't kid himself, the money he had was sufficient appeal to anyone. He'd known Melissa had married him for love as he hadn't had two cents back then. Yet she'd never complained. She'd delighted in their good fortune when the software had begun to take off. Now he was too cynical to believe in love with money and fame so enticingly included.

"Come on, Juan and Pablo, let's go find your rooms. You might want to take a short nap, too," Stacey said, heading for the door.

"I don't want to take a nap," Juan said, racing after her. Pablo lagged behind a little, looking over his shoulder at his father in appeal.

"I'll come up with you," Luis said. Pablo clearly needed some extra encouragement in the strange setting.

Juan was already racing up the stairs when Luis and Pablo caught up with Stacey.

"These stairs are so wide. The extravagance of space is not what I'm used to in New York," she said, admiring the staircase.

"This was built in the 1920s when lavish styles were the rage. It's a solid house."

"Lovely." She didn't say anything else. Or try to flirt or make mention of his grandmother's room assignments. Her serenity fascinated him. So far he'd never seen her flustered.

The third floor held several bedrooms and a large playroom. Memories crowded in as he surveyed the old toys and games and books. The chairs were way too small for him now, but once upon a time they'd been perfect.

"What fun we'll have here if it rains," Stacey said to the boys as she wandered to the shelves and looked at the books. Most were in Spanish, but there were a few English versions. Board games were neatly boxed. There were blocks, and puzzles, and trucks and dolls. It was perfect for children of various ages.

"Their room will be next door," Luis said. He felt awkward. She should be staying near the children. His grandmother knew that. He didn't want to give Stacey any false impressions or ideas. She was a temporary nanny for his children, nothing more. If she read anything into Abuela Marie's room assignment, he'd have to set her straight.

"Fabulous. If they wake up early, they can play quietly until it's time for breakfast," she said, following him into the bedroom that held twin beds.

The boys came in, curious to see their bedroom. Juan bounced on the bed, then flopped down.

"I think we should wash our face and hands and lie down while I read you a story," Stacey said as one of the maids brought up their suitcases.

"I'll leave you to it, then," Luis said, anxious to escape before he started thinking along the lines of his grandmother. It was interesting to see Stacey's interaction with Juan and Pablo. He was used to Hannah, loving yet a bit staid. Stacey made everything seem like an adventure.

Luis went down to the second floor and to his room. His things had already been unpacked and put away. Eyeing the bed, he considered lying down himself, but knew he'd be asleep in no time. He wanted to stay awake to adjust to European time as quickly as possible. Going to the windows, he looked out on the gardens. They were lovely, in full bloom. He opened the window, stepping out onto the porch that wrapped around the villa. The fragrance that filled the air also brought many memories.

How many summers had he spent here? A dozen at least. His father had led a busy life, and hadn't wanted young children along, complicating things. His sister had enjoyed the summers. He had too, once he'd reconciled himself to staying. As a teenager, though, he'd rebelled more than once.

Turning, he started back into his room when his eye caught the open French doors next to his. That was the room where Stacey would be sleeping. He frowned. Maybe he should suggest a different room for her.

For the first time since Melissa's death he considered what it would be like to marry again. He'd never meet anyone like Melissa. But it would be better if he could share the raising of his children with someone who would

love them as much as he did. Maybe even have another child or two. He thought he'd like a little girl. One with blonde curls and a sunny smile.

He took one last look at the garden and went back into the bedroom. The fatigue from the flight was rattling his mind. He had work to do, not fantasies to dream.

Stacey settled the boys down on one bed and brought out one of her books from her tote. She lay down beside them and opened the big picture book to read. They were all crowded together with scarcely any room to move, but the boys didn't complain, eager to hear the story. By the time she reached the end, both of them were sound asleep.

She covered them with a light blanket and quietly left the room, leaving the door ajar so she could hear them. She didn't want them upset or scared when they woke in a strange place.

Entering the playroom, she walked around, studying it thoughtfully. This was where Luis had spent his summers. Had he missed his parents or been so thoroughly indulged by his grandparents he hadn't had a chance to miss them? He'd mentioned a sister. Stacey supposed she would also be attending the birthday gathering. Would their parents?

She went to the window to look at the sea. She couldn't wait to get out there. She hoped the boys loved it as much as she did. What a great way to spend the vacation. Idly she reviewed her meeting with Luis's grandmother. She wondered if she'd misread her room assignment. She smiled at the memory of the look on Luiss' face. He'd looked horrified.

She almost giggled. She wasn't really looking for a husband—she loved her work. What else could she do that combined her love for travel with her enjoyment of

children? She'd never dreamed as a girl in West Virginia that she'd get to travel the world and stay in premier vacation locations. Vacation Nannies had only been in business five years, but she'd seen so much of the world that she wouldn't trade it for anything.

Well, maybe a home and family one day. But not this summer.

Checking on the boys, she was reassured they'd sleep for some time. Enough time, she hoped, for her to take a quick shower and maybe find some more coffee.

Descending the stairs to the second floor, she looked both ways. Which way to the rose room? Several doors were open, several closed. She walked down the hall to her right, looking into the rooms. A gold room, a blue room. This one had wallpaper of tiny little flowers with yellow and green the predominant colors. There was an old-fashioned bath with a huge claw-foot tub, wide sink and opened windows, letting in the sun and sea air.

The doors to the other side were closed. She tapped lightly on one, waited and when she heard no response opened the door. This was as lovely as the others, but more a taupe color than rose.

She tapped on the next door and a second later Luis opened it. He'd removed his jacket and tie and loosened the color of his shirt. She stared at him for a moment, taken aback by the casualness. He'd been all business since she'd met him. She liked the slightly disheveled look. It made him all the more appealing.

Forget it, she admonished herself. She'd never have thought that if not for the grandmother's room assignment. He was just one in a long line of high-powered employers she'd work for over the next few weeks and likely never see again.

"I guess the next room is mine," she said.

"No one showed you?" He frowned. "My grand-mother's usually known for her hospitality."

"Well, I was up with the boys, who are fast asleep now. I thought a quick shower and change of clothes would be in order. When they waken, we'll go to the beach. What time are the meals? Do they eat upstairs in the playroom?"

"Lunch is at noon. Dinner's at seven. And the boys will probably eat with everyone else. I always did. Once the entire family gathers, it's unlikely we'll have one table that'll hold everyone. But we'll all still eat together. As long as the weather is nice, we'll use the terrace."

"I'll make sure they're ready for each meal."

"Stacey." Luis paused a moment.

"Yes?"

"Don't read anything into the room arrangement."

She almost wanted to challenge him on what he could possibly mean. But that would be silly—they both knew what he was talking about.

"Don't worry, your bachelorhood is safe with me. I have no designs on you."

She walked down the hall to the next room and opened the door slowly. Peering in, she was enchanted with it. Rose walls, a deep rose carpet and white duvet on the bed made it look fresh and pretty. And pink was her fa-vorite color, in all shades.

She waved to Luis, still standing at his door, watch-ing her, and entered, closing the door behind her. She wasn't sure whether to be insulted or amused by his com-ment. Did he have so many women chasing him that he thought all were? Granted, there was that pesky aware-ness of him as a very virile man that flared every time she saw him, but she'd been around some of the world's most exciting men—it was a mere aberration. Once she

got a good night's sleep, she'd be back to viewing him merely as the father of her charges.

Time to check out her room for the next three weeks. She noticed her suitcase near the door. When she picked it up, it was too light to contain clothes. Opening the wardrobe, she saw her dresses had been hung up. A quick look in the dresser showed the rest of her things. Nice to be pampered while working, she thought. There was an en suite bath on the side. The huge claw-foot tub dominated the room, but a modern shower was tucked in one corner.

Once showered and in fresh clothes, Stacey went back upstairs to await the boys' awakening. It would be lunchtime soon, and after they ate, they could go to the beach.

Lunch was served alfresco on the veranda, with bread and cold cuts and spreads suitable for a wide variety of tastes. Stacey prepared sandwiches for herself and the boys and led them to a small table near the gardens. There was a larger table closer to the house, but she thought for this first meal they would feel more comfortable not sitting with strangers. She sat between them, to help when they needed it and to referee if required.

When Abuela Maria came from the house she stopped by the table to ask the boys if they wouldn't rather eat at the long table set nearby, where Sophia was heading.

Pablo looked at Stacey with stricken eyes.

"I think this would suit us better," Stacey said, smiling in response to his stricken look. "Once they're more comfortable with everyone, then I think they'll fit right in. Maybe in a day or two?"

"Perhaps tomorrow. I want them to enjoy their visit, and want to hear all they're doing. But children take a little time to adjust," the older woman said with a smile to her great-grandsons. "We want you to join us as well,"

she said to Stacey. With another smile, she went to sit at the larger table with Sophia.

"She talks funny," Juan said quietly, his eyes still studying his *abuela*.

"She's speaking English with a Spanish accent, as a concession to you two who don't speak Spanish. Maybe you can learn some words in her language while we're here and surprise her. She'd like that," Stacey explained. "I'll teach you, how's that?"

"I don't want to learn stuff, I want to play," Juan said, taking a bite of his sandwich. The he looked up. "Except learn to swim. Daddy said he'd teach me."

"Ah, *nadar*," Stacey said with a nod.

"Huh?"

"*Nadar* is Spanish for to swim. So if you want to do that, you need to say it in Spanish," Stacey said.

"*Nadar*. Can we go after we eat?"

"*Sí*."

"See?"

Stacey nodded. "*Sí* is Spanish for yes."

She caught sight of Luis coming from the house. He looked refreshed and amazing in a polo shirt and khaki slacks. Her throat went dry. When he went to the buffet to fill his plate and then went to sit at the main table, it was all she could do to drag her eyes away. She wished she could check her hair, make sure her lipstick was still on.

Placing his plate on the main table, he came over to them.

"Not eating with the rest of us?"

"I thought it best for the boys to get used to things slowly," she said. "Did you want them there?"

"Not necessarily. I trust your judgment." He looked at the twins. "And they seem to be doing okay. For a while

there I was afraid the entire vacation would be full of complaints and comments about returning home."

"We're going to have too much fun to think about returning home. We're going to *la playa* after lunch—will you be joining us?"

"I have some work to do. I should warn you, the boys don't know how to swim."

"*Nadar*, Daddy," Pablo said. "We're going to learn to *nadar*, if we say it in Spanish."

"Ah, very good. So *usted irá a la playa a aprender nadar.*"

Juan looked at him in confusion. "What?"

"He said we'll go to the beach to learn to swim," Stacey said, smiling at the child. "Your daddy already speaks Spanish. We'll have to surprise him, too."

"Aren't you going to teach me to *nadar*, Daddy?" Juan asked.

"If I get done with my work today. Otherwise maybe tomorrow," Luis said.

He returned to the main table. Stacey couldn't hear the conversation but she could tell from her posture that Maria was scolding her grandson. She hid a grin. The businessman didn't look like anything could sway him, but for a second she could see the little boy he'd once been, listening respectfully to his *abuela*.

Luis listened politely to his grandmother chiding him for staying away so long.

"I'm not getting younger, you need to visit more often," she said in rapid Spanish.

"I have been away too long. But it's not easy to travel with children."

"They are old enough now, certainly." She looked at the boys and her expression softened. "They remind me

of you and your sister when you came to visit. I love having children in the house." She studied the three at the table near the flowers and nodded. "I think they like their nanny very much. But they should be with you. You work too long, this vacation should be about family and not work. Spend time with them, Luis."

"I will. There are only a few things to see to, then I can. And they have Stacey. She'll see they have a good visit," he conceded, looking over. For a moment he wished Stacey had brought them to the main table. He watched as even Pablo seemed captivated by whatever it was she was saying. His shy little boy was warming to the temporary nanny. He hoped both boys enjoyed the visit. He did need to make time for them, but until he could, he was sure they were fine.

The beach was wide and white, the sand fine and clean when the trio headed out after lunch. The Mediterranean Sea stretched as far as the eye could see, various shades of turquoise and blue. A soft breeze blew off the water, keeping the temperature comfortable. One of the servants had set up a wide umbrella for shade, but the two little boys didn't want to sit in the sand. They raced to the water, and splashed in, stopping when the water reached their knees.

Stacey dropped the towels and ran after them, grabbing a hand each and slowly encouraging them to walk farther into the water. It was shallow and even when they had walked out twenty feet the water was not too deep for the boys. They loved splashing, running to the beach and back into the water.

"I want to swim," Juan called.

Pablo stopped near Stacey, and reached out to hold her hand. "It's scary," he said.

"Only because you don't know how to swim yet. It'll be fun. Juan, come here, we'll begin."

"Daddy said he'd teach me," Juan said, standing near the shore studying the water with trepidation.

"When he can, I'm sure he'll come out with us, but we can get some basics out of the way and surprise him," she called.

A moment later he waded out to her. The water wasn't even waist high on the boys.

"First we'll practice putting our faces in the water," she said, kneeling down to be more at their level. She showed them how and both boys dutifully put their faces in the water for a split second. Juan came up with a wide grin, Pablo looked uncertain.

"Let's do it again, this time blow bubbles. Let's see who can blow bubbles the longest."

Several minutes passed as they all blew bubbles. Gradually Pablo became more comfortable. Stacey was delighted when he finally raised his face with a grin on it. "I blew them the longest," he said proudly.

"Indeed you did, sweetie. You're our bubble champ."

"I can do that," Juan said, taking a deep breath and plunging beneath the water. Bubbles popped on the surface. When he finished he stood up and grinned. "Now am I the longest?"

"It's a tie," she said with a laugh. These boys were fun.

A moment later she was surprised to see Luis striding across the sand, wearing swim trunks, a towel slung around his neck. His wide shoulders and muscular chest were already tanned. Where had he been to acquire that? she wondered. She'd thought he worked all the time.

Catching herself staring, she turned and focused on the boys, suddenly conscious of the bikini she wore.

Perfectly suitable for the sea, it was still revealing. Not that children noticed, but there was nothing child-like about Luis Aldivista.

"Daddy!" Pablo ran out of the water to greet him.

"I thought you had work," Stacey called, definitely not having expected him. What was she trying to do, send him back inside?

"My grandmother does not have internet service, and she was not willing for me to tie up her phone for long-distance calls. She very patiently explained the concept of vacations to me," he said with a rueful smile.

Stacey was captivated by that smile. It took years off his looks, making him seem like a carefree younger version, out for a good time.

"The boys are delighted to have you here," she said. Juan was already jumping up and down beside him, begging his father to teach him to swim.

"Shall I leave them with you?" she asked. It would be a great for him to spend time with his sons. She'd only be in the way.

"No, stay. One on one's a better ratio."

"I want to swim," Juan called again.

"How about Stacey and I teach you both at the same time?" Luis asked, dropping his towel and walking into the water.

Stacey could have easily forgotten the children and feasted her eyes on him for the rest of the afternoon. His wide shoulders tapered to slim hips. His muscular chest seemed out of place with a man who commanded a software development firm and worked inside most of the day. This man seriously kept himself in shape!

She needed to get a grip. She was there solely for the boys, not to enjoy the physique of her reluctant employer. Concentrate on teaching the boys to swim, she told her-

self firmly. Easier said than done with a tantalizing male so near.

As the afternoon wore on, she was able to forget about ogling Luis Aldivista and enjoy the fun the children were having with two adults devoting their attention solely on them. Before long Pablo surprised them all by swimming by himself. He happily paddled between Stacey and Luis, kicking and splashing, but definitely moving through the water.

Juan tried, but he was too impatient and when he couldn't he'd slap the water and pout.

"You have the magic touch," Luis said after several unsuccessful attempts to teach him. "I'll work with Pablo, on refining his technique, and you see if you can get Juan to the same stage."

"Okay."

Luis watched for a moment as Juan floundered around again. Stacey had a world of patience. She laughed when his son did, but never made fun of him or belittled his efforts.

"Daddy, can I swim again?" Pablo asked. Luis stopped watching Stacey and focused on his son. But one part of him was always aware of where she was and how she and Juan were doing.

She looked amazing in that bikini. Her body was curvy, trim and feminine. It'd been a long time since he'd seen such a scantily dressed woman. He swallowed once when his libido rose. He needed to focus on his children and not on their nanny. It had nothing to do with anything but the vacation atmosphere, the difference between being here and back in New York and working. Under any other circumstances, he would never have met Stacey. To think of anything but his children was futile.

Deliberately turning his back, he encouraged Pablo as his son practiced what he'd learned.

As the afternoon waned, the boys grew more and more proficient. They soon were swimming between Luis and Stacey, who moved back a few feet each time.

Luis realized what she was doing but didn't call her on it. The boys were learning and that was important. But more importantly he was enjoying himself. When Juan and Pablo launched themselves again to swim toward Stacey, Luis tried to remember the last time he'd spent the afternoon with his sons. Nothing popped into mind.

"I winned, I winned!" Pablo yelled, splashing in the water as he jumped up and down in excitement.

"I winned last time," Juan said when he reached Stacey.

Luis was proud of them. His heart lurched when he realized he'd almost missed this special milestone in their lives. The day they'd learned to swim.

Not only was he here for that event, he was having more fun than he'd had in years.

"Ready, set, go!" Stacey yelled, and the two began swimming furiously toward him. His throat almost closed. How close he'd come to missing all this. What if his grandmother had not minded him tying up her phone for hours?

He held out his arms like a barrier. Their techniques were atrocious, but their enthusiasm and excitement couldn't be measured. His laughter rang out when they both touched his hands at the same time.

Stacey grinned at the sound of Luis's laughter. Who would have known the man had it in him? She'd been so surprised when he'd joined them, and even more so that he'd joined in their play. It would mean a lot to the

boys to have their father's attention. And if his involve-ment these last few hours were anything to go on, he'd actually enjoyed himself too.

Maybe there was a chance for him after all. Sometimes she thought devotion to business was pure habit. Could Luis break that habit and give more of his time to his children? She'd love to see that.

The hours passed quickly. Stacey wasn't used to being with the parents if they spent time with their children. Usually she was hired to keep them entertained—away from the parents. When the parents wanted their chil-dren, she was given free time. So she wasn't entirely sure how to deal with this. But as long as the fun continued, she'd be right in there.

She tried to focus on the boys and their delight in their newly learned skill, but one part of her was attuned to their disturbing father. He was definitely a cut above most of the men she knew. And for just a second or two she wished their business relationship might be a tad dif-ferent as well.

Other families came to the beach from nearby villas. Stacey saw them watch the four of them in the water and wondered if they thought them a family. Her coloring was similar to that of the boys, yet they looked too much like their father to mistake their parentage. They'd already had that misconception once. For a moment she let her-self dream about mothering these children. They were a bit exuberant and unruly, but she had dealt with difficult children. She would do her best to channel their energy into healthy pursuits and hope their natural exuberance could be contained while they still grew and learned.

What would it be like to become their mother?

She almost dropped Juan when the thought popped into her head. Hoping Luis could't read minds, she tried

to forget the idea. Time to firmly squelch any thoughts along those lines.

By the time they were ready to return to the villa, both boys were tired and hungry.

Stacey was glad to get back to the house. Once there, she hoped Luis would find other activities to occupy his time. She'd grown more and more conscious of him as the afternoon had worn on. Gone was the austere businessman. He looked almost as carefree as his twins.

It didn't help that he looked so fabulous in his swim trunks. Or that he was strong enough to carry both boys when they clung to him. Or that when he looked at her from time to time and grinned, her heart flipped over and then raced. Her skin felt tingly every time she bumped against him and the longer the afternoon wore on, the more concerned she grew at the fascination that grew by leaps and bounds.

She had the urge to brush her fingers over that tanned skin, feel the strength of those muscles with deliberate intent, not just the accident touch of skin to skin.

Oh, man, major jet-lag. It had to be. She needed a good night's sleep to get back her equilibrium.

When they got back to the villa, Stacey felt like she could sleep for a week. The sunshine and water had been invigorating, but now she was feeling the lack of sleep and the pleasant relaxation from spending time in the sea. She'd love to lie down for a few minutes. If dinner was not until seven, maybe she and the boys could take a quick nap.

She helped the boys take a short bath to get rid of the salt water, towel-dried their hair and gave them each a picture book to look at while she took her own shower. Dressed in slacks and a cotton top, she rejoined them a short time later.

"Want me to read a book?" she asked, pleased they

had both remained in their beds with the books she'd given.

A chorus of "Yes!" filled the air. Smiling, she snuggled next to Pablo, Juan jumping over to join them. In less than five minutes both boys were asleep. Stacey relaxed and closed her eyes. She'd rest just for a moment herself. She hoped her internal alarm would wake them in time for dinner.

Just before seven Luis went to find the boys. Dinner would be served shortly. Alfresco again, which suited him to a *T*. He relished the warm climate, the freshness of the air. Memories of his summers spent here at the villa crowded his mind. He'd loved the casual manner his grandparents had allowed, bringing him and his sister into line only if needed. Life had been easier then.

He took the steps two at a time and in seconds paused at the door to the boys' bedroom. Both his sons and Stacey were fast asleep. The boys looked angelic and so did Stacey, her skin lightly pink. He knew she'd slathered sun screen on herself and the boys, and was grateful she had done so. Pablo had his head resting on her shoulder. Juan had his arms flung wide, one across Stacey's stomach. A book lay across her chest, rising and falling with her breathing.

He felt a catch in his breath as he studied the scene. His sons with their blond hair, Stacey with hers only a shade lighter. It looked right. His boys were missing a lot, growing up without a mother. The softness of a woman's touch, the gentle nature that would strive to teach manners and caring and values. He'd been surprised how easily Stacey had fit in. Hannah had been with him for six years, yet he had never seen her cuddle his boys, lie down with them to read or talk or reassure. How had

Stacey captured their trust so they would lay their heads on her shoulders and feel so safe and cared for?

Hannah did a good job raising them. A mother would be even better. When had they grown so big? So often work kept him late, so the boys were usually in bed for the night when he returned home and he'd see them like this—asleep, looking angelic. Six wasn't a great age, but the years seemed to have flown by.

Melissa would have adored these twins. The two of them should be raising their children. He frowned, trying to picture her face, trying to imagine her with the boys. But the only image that rose was Stacey laughing in the sea, Stacey bending closer when reading to them on the plane. Stacey napping with them. They'd all had fun this afternoon. It was the happiest he'd seen the boys in years. And their normally wild behavior had not been evident. They had listened to Stacey.

He would, too, he thought wryly, if she made everything in life as much fun as she did for the boys.

Maybe he'd made a mistake in hiring an older nanny. He could already see the change in his boys from being with someone young like Stacey. Not that he'd trade Hannah for anything. But he had to find more time to spend with them. In only a dozen years they'd be grown and off to college and life on their own.

And where would Stacey be in twelve years? he wondered. It was an odd career—to care for other people's children for short stretches of time. What compelled a pretty woman like her to do that rather than raise her own children?

He checked his watch. If they were to eat with the rest of the family tonight, they needed to get up now. But he was reluctant to wake them. He committed the sight of

them all sleeping to memory. One he'd cherish in the years ahead.

Turning, he decided to let them sleep. He'd ask his grandmother if they could have a snack later if they woke. The image of Stacey cuddled up with his sons didn't fade but remained clearly in his mind throughout the evening.

With the boys absent from dinner, his grandmother spoke in Spanish.

"I want to make sure you don't forget our language," she told him with a smile.

"Never. I use it sometimes in the States," Luis told her.

Sophia asked about his work and he explained the projects currently under way, some of the difficulties in the current market. He kept it brief, suspecting she was asking from a sense of good manners rather than strong interest.

"And your sons, how are they doing with no mother?" the elderly woman asked a short time later.

"Well enough. Our regular nanny, Hannah, has been with them since birth. So they have stability. She takes good care of them." He wouldn't touch on what a handful they were, or the more and more frequent complaints of the nanny that they might need more discipline—especially when out in public.

"Stacey's only hired for this vacation?" his grandmother asked. "I don't believe I've heard of temporary nannies before."

"She's part owner of a firm called Vacation Nannies. Their sole function is to watch children while families are on vacation. The service doesn't come cheap, but she came highly recommended and was available at the last

minute when I discovered Hannah would not be swayed from her fear of flying."

"She seems to be a lovely young woman. And the boys respond well to her," Abuela Maria said, taking another bite of the paella they'd been served. "And she speaks Spanish."

"Which she's endeavoring to teach the boys, at least a word here and there," Luis said.

He'd been remiss in not teaching the boys himself. Their heritage was the same as his. What if they wanted to come spend the summer in Spain one year? He'd definitely see to Spanish lessons when they returned home.

Melissa hadn't spoken Spanish. He thought about their only visit to Spain. Melissa had not enjoyed it as much has he'd hoped. Not that anyone had been rude or unkind. But she hadn't fit in and it had showed. Would that have changed had she lived? She had been in her element in New York. Maybe she hadn't been as versatile as he'd remembered.

"How long have you known her?" Maria asked.

"I hired her the day before we left."

"And you trust your children to a stranger?" Sophia asked, shocked.

"I'm here, we're all here. I doubt she could snatch them and get far. Besides, I checked references."

"Don't worry, Sophia, it's the way they do things in America. Tell me more about your apartment," his grandmother asked. "It's not the one I visited, is it?"

Glad to get off the subject of Stacey, he complied. He was proud of the new and larger apartment he now had. A sign of success. His only regret was that he didn't spend any more time it in than he had the older one. Business was a demanding mistress.

After discussing the amenities and proximity to a park

for some minutes, his grandmother frowned. "You work too hard. It sounds as if Hannah has sole responsibility for your twins. When do you have time for your children?"

"Weekends, mostly." When he wasn't working.

She nodded. "I suspected as much. That'll be changed here. I invited everyone to visit and have fun. It's a holiday, so no work."

"I can't operate that way, Abuela. I have responsibilities."

"You can. You can choose not to work." She met his gaze with an unflinching one of her own.

He wasn't going to argue with her. Maybe there was a smidgen of truth there. He found he could forget Melissa and her sudden death if he was wrapped up in work. It had become habit. He loved the challenge of programming to meet all needs. His initial grief had long passed, yet his passion for work remained

"What a perfect opportunity for you to show them the land of their heritage. And you'll have the help of a young assistant so it won't be hard, watching two rambunctious children," his grandmother said with a smile.

Luis knew when he was beat. He nodded. He'd have to find time when he could check in at the office when his grandmother wouldn't know.

"Tomorrow's market day. You know how you loved that as a child."

And maybe there was an internet café in the village now, he thought.

"An excellent idea. We can get an early start and be back by lunch."

He'd have Stacey take the boys while he connected with the office. The perfect arrangement.

CHAPTER THREE

STACEY woke to darkness and two warm bodies pressed against her. Slowly she untangled herself and rose. She felt her way to the door of the playroom and flipped on its light. The illumination gave enough light into the bedroom for her to see the boys, sprawled together, sound asleep. She took a light blanket from the second bed and covered them. Checking her watch, she noted it was almost ten o'clock. She'd slept right through dinner.

Should she wake the boys? A good night's sleep would be the best thing for them. Yet they could wake soon and be hungry. Maybe she'd find her way to the kitchen and see what she could scavenge for a late supper. Crackers and peanut butter would keep in the playroom if they awoke later.

She went to her room to freshen up, then walked down the main stairs. There were lights on and the sound of conversation from the main salon. She headed there.

"Ah, you're awake, and hungry, I'm sure," Senora Aldivista said when she saw Stacey. "Luis, show her the kitchen and help her get something to eat. Are the boys awake?"

"They're still sleeping. But I thought I should take something up for them in case they wake later in the night," Stacey said.

"Excellent idea. There're crackers and peanut butter in the pantry. A good snack if they awaken and you'd not have to come back downstairs."

"If you tell me where the kitchen is, I'll find it," she said with a glance at Luis. He was already standing and walking toward her. She didn't want him to interrupt his visit to cater to her.

"I'll show you. Might have one or two of those crackers myself," he said.

He led the way down the hall, through the dining room and into the spacious kitchen. Flipping on lights, he went straight to the large double-door refrigerator and opened it.

"We had paella for dinner. Ahh, there was some left. It's easily warmed up. I don't know if the boys would like it as much as peanut butter."

"I can manage. I didn't mean to take you away from your grandmother," Stacey said, reaching for the plate piled high with the saffron-tinted rice. Her fingers brushed his and she almost dropped the dish with the spark that seemed to leap from his hand to hers.

"Microwave's over here," he said, leading the way.

He had not felt the jolt if his demeanor was anything to go by. Stacey took a breath and held on to the plate, hoping she didn't look as foolish as she felt.

She placed it in the microwave and he punched in the time. In only a couple of minutes the fragrant aroma of the meal filled the kitchen.

"Do you want to eat in here or the dining room?" Luis asked.

"Here. And you don't have to stay with me, I'll be fine." She felt nervous around him. Probably from her fantasies at the beach. She was a competent adult, she could fend for herself.

"My grandmother was saying she was about ready to retire for the night. Sophia's obviously tired and I think Abuela Maria didn't want her to feel she had to remain up any later."

"And you, how are you holding up? Did you nap this afternoon?" Stacey asked.

"I'm tired, too. But I want to adjust to this time as quickly as possible. I'll be heading up soon. A good night's sleep and I'll be fine. Do you think the boys will sleep through the night?"

Stacey nodded, sitting on one of the stools at the island in the center of the kitchen. She took a bite of the paella and almost purred with pleasure. It was delicious. "I'll have to get this recipe. I've had paella before, but never this good."

Luis leaned against the counter opposite the island and crossed his arms across his chest, watching her as she ate. Stacey glanced at him from time to time, noting he looked tired.

"You don't have to wait for me," she said, finding it more and more difficult to eat with his eyes on her. She should have refreshed her make-up, not just pulled a brush through her hair.

"You'll be finished soon enough. Tomorrow I thought I'd take you and the boys to the village. The weekly market sets up early in the morning. I remember it from when I was a kid, visiting. Everything you can think of is for sale there. I think they'll like exploring the different booths."

"Sounds fun."

"I need to find an internet café. You can manage them on your own, right?"

She nodded. She personally thought the boys would love to have their father accompany them, telling them

about when he'd been a boy. Maybe she could find out more to tell them herself.

"Tell me about your visits to the market in the past," she said.

He looked startled at her request.

"So I can tell the boys. Maybe they'll make the same kind of memories."

"The earliest I remember was when my grandparents had to take me. It seemed so foreign to the sterile supermarkets in the States. Later Isabella and I were old enough to go on our own. It's a weekly market, so we'd cajole our grandparents—separately so the other wouldn't know—to give us money to spend. I liked the wooden carvings best. I had an entire fleet of boats one summer."

She enjoyed listening to him talk while she ate. He started with the memories he had of the weekly market, then moved on to other aspects of his visits that held lasting memories. She was finished before he wound down, and could have sat and listened to him all night.

"You're done. And I've bored you enough," he said, noting her empty plate.

"Never. I can share those memories with your sons when we're on our own. They need that connection with family, you know. It builds closer ties. You should tell them stories about your summers when you are all together."

"Our family's pretty scattered. It's hard to build close ties when we rarely see each other," he said.

"All the more reason to make sure that when you do get together you make shared memories to carry you until you get together again."

"Are members of your family close?"

"There's only my sister and, yes, we're close. We share an apartment in Brooklyn."

"Is she a Vacation Nanny?"

Stacey nodded. "We started this business together."

"Where is she now?"

"Her last assignment was on a cruise in Alaska. She was due home today. She'll probably be off again before I get home. Summer's our busiest time."

"No other family?"

Stacey shook her head, picked up her dish and carried it to the sink. As she ran hot water over it, she glanced at Luis. His sandy hair gleamed beneath the light. His eyes studied her. The fluttering in her midsection was not something she wanted to contend with.

"If you show me the peanut butter and crackers, I'll make up some snacks for the boys and then head back upstairs. I thought I'd spend tonight with them in the other bed. I like a little more room, but if they wake in the night I don't want them to feel alone in a strange place."

"They'll probably sleep through," he said. He really didn't know. Hannah would know.

"Probably," Stacey concurred.

Gathering things needed for a midnight snack, Stacey tried to focus on what she wanted to take upstairs and not on the man who was close enough to touch. She had worked for many fathers before and had never felt this awareness. Though usually she got her directions from the mother. It was going to be a long three weeks if she couldn't get past this.

The next morning dawned bright and beautiful. The boys slept through the night but were wide awake by seven and bouncing around on their bed. Stacey opened her

eyes and watched them for a moment before they realized she was awake.

"*Buenos dias*," she said.

"What's that?" Juan asked.

"Good morning," Pablo said.

"*Sí*, that is good morning in Spanish." She sat up, pushing the light blanket off. She still wore her clothes from last night and couldn't wait for a quick shower and change.

The boys practiced the phrase for several minutes, then Juan said, "I'm hungry."

"We'll get dressed and you two can play for a few minutes while I get dressed, then we'll go find breakfast," Stacey said.

"I want to eat now!" Juan said.

"First, it's impolite not to have fresh clothes when going to breakfast with your hostess. Second, a bit of patience doesn't come amiss."

"Huh?"

Pablo jumped on the bed. "I want to eat now."

Stacey fixed them both with a stern eye, which was hard to do when they were so adorable. "What did I say?"

"Get dressed first," Juan said, settling down.

"And?" she continued.

"Wait for you to get dressed," Pablo said. "Will you be fast?"

"Quick as a bunny."

When they went downstairs a short time later, they heard the murmur of voices in the dining room Stacey led the boys there.

"Ah, *buenos dias*," Abuela Maria said. "Did you sleep well?"

"*Sí*," Juan said, beaming. Pablo hung back beside Stacey, his eyes wide as he surveyed the two elderly

ladies eating breakfast. The large dining table dominated the room. A carved buffet held several dishes and a gleaming silver coffee pot.

"*Muy bien*, you are learning Spanish," Abuela Maria said with a matching smile. "Help yourself to breakfast. We made an English breakfast as well as our own rolls and breads."

Stacey spoke softly to the boys, reminding them of the manners they'd best show if they wanted to go to the beach later.

The boys made short work of their breakfast and finished before Stacey. Their behavior, however, couldn't be faulted. She was relieved. Sometimes she wondered how Hannah managed—they were a handful!

"Can we go to the beach?" Pablo asked. "I want to swim again."

"How about a visit to the local market first?" Luis said, coming in just in time to hear Pablo's request.

"Hi, Daddy. We ate our breakfast already. You're late," Juan said, jumping up to run to hug Luis.

Pablo followed suit.

Stacey smiled at the picture of the three of them. The boys still had a lot of growing to do to reach their father's height, and for a moment she had a pang that she wouldn't see them when they grew up. What would they be like?

Often she wished she could follow the children she spent time with. A few families asked for her each summer. For those she could keep track of how the children grew and changed, but it was the others where she wondered from time to time what the families were up to and how "her kids" were doing.

"What's a market?" Pablo asked.

"You'll like it, it's like an open-air department store,"

Luis said after he'd greeted everyone. He'd finished his breakfast earlier and was now ready to leave.

"Be back by one. We'll have lunch then. Your cousins are arriving today," Maria said.

The drive to the village was quick. The market was held in the center of the town at the square and the streets were lined with parked cars. There were display booths back to back in lines crossing the square. Already the market was crowded with women shopping for fruit and vegetables, tourists perusing the craft goods and other items for sale.

Luis parked on a side street, getting one of the last available spaces. "I forgot how crowded it gets on market day. Many of the locals do their grocery shopping for fresh produce. And there are always the tourists, new each week, who crowd the area, looking for bargains."

"What fun. I love these kinds of markets. Juan and Pablo, we will have a *muy bien* time here," Stacey said.

"*Sí señorita.* Can we go now?" Juan said.

Luis hid a smile at his son's mangling of the language as he turned in the seat and looked at the twins. "You stay with Stacey, no wandering away. You could get lost and with few people here speaking English, it could take a long time to be found."

"I'll watch them closely," Stacey murmured. "And where will you be? You're not joining us?"

"I need to find an internet café and get some work done. If I finish in time, I'll find you. Otherwise we meet back here in three hours."

"You should come with them. These are experiences to be shared." She'd seen this too many times to be surprised by it, but she really wished parents would spend time with their children. The years were racing by.

"I've told you some of my experiences, you can con-

vey them to the boys," he said, opening the car door and reaching in the back for his laptop.

She opened hers and looked at him across the roof of the sedan. "It's not the same."

Luis frowned. "Work comes first."

"Family should come first," she countered, then wished she'd kept quiet. It was so not her place to give advice to her employer.

He glared at her. "Easy for you to say with no family to speak of. But I have to earn a living to provide for my family."

She should keep quiet. It was not her business, but some imp had her returning, "You have a gazillion dollars from your software. If you never worked another day the boys would not starve," she bit out, frustrated he didn't see what was right before his eyes. Two precious children wanting to spend time with their only parent.

"Checking up on me?" he asked in a silky tone, his eyes narrowed in sudden suspicion.

"We do reference checks as well, you know. We don't want to be stiffed for the bill."

Stacey opened the back door on her side and Pablo got out of the car. A moment later Juan followed. "Okay, kiddos, let's go exploring." She didn't give Luis another look but slipped her shoulder-bag strap over her head and reached for the boys' hands.

The market was like a festival. There were people everywhere, laughing and talking. Small groups catching up on gossip since last week. The vendors called out tantalizing enticements for people to stop at their booths. She eyed the fresh fruit, buying three bananas to share with the boys later. They wandered down one row and looked at everything. The next row had a woodcarver's booth, with toys and frames and elegant furnishings.

"Did you make all this?" she asked the vendor as the boys looked at the wooden toys.

The man selling the items was old and wrinkled, his hands gnarled and scarred. In one hand was a wicked-looking knife, the other had a delicate humming bird, which was almost finished.

"It gives an old man something to do," he said. "Treat your boys to a toy, *señora*. Make us all happy today."

She laughed. "Not a bad idea." Switching to English, she asked the twins if they'd like any of the toys. Both picked cars. The price was very low and Stacey asked about the almost finished humming bird.

"If you wait a few minutes, it'll be ready to fly off to your home," the man said, resuming work.

Stacey and the boys watched as he deftly carved the last of the wings. Though wood, she could almost feel the flutter of the delicate wings. He polished the bird with a rag and oil and then studied it a moment.

"It's lovely," she said. A delightful souvenir of her Spanish holiday.

He wrapped all the items in newspaper and put them in a bag for them. Stacey also chose a couple of carved wooden frames, and lingered a long time over a small table with inset tiles. No way to get that home, but it was lovely.

"I want to play with my car," Juan said when they walked away from the booth.

"Better to wait until we return to the villa," Stacey said. "What if you dropped it and someone stepped on it before you got home? Or it got lost?"

"Can we have something to eat?" Pablo asked. "I'm hungry."

"Sure thing, sweetie. Then we'll see more of the mar-

ket." She pulled out the bananas and each ate theirs as they strolled along.

"Everyone speaks Spanish and they talk too fast," Juan complained.

"When you're in America, you speak English fast and Spanish visitors would have a hard time understanding you," Stacey said. "Maybe your dad will teach you more Spanish and soon you'll be talking like a native."

"What's a native?" Pablo asked.

"A person born in a place," she replied. "Look at the pictures in this booth."

They commented on some of the craft booths they passed. The twins asked a couple of times to buy something, but Stacey reminded them of their cars and they stopped.

It was getting closer to the time to meet Luis.

"I'm thirsty," Pablo said.

"Then let's see if we can find a place to get a drink," Stacey suggested. The day was growing warmer and the initial novelty of the market was waning. The boys had been good enough as they'd explored, but she suspected their interest had been exhausted.

They walked briskly to the edge of the square and looked around for a café where they could sit and get something cool to drink. Slowly they walked around the perimeter, finally spotting a place with outdoor table and chairs. It was a beautiful day and she didn't want to miss any of it by being inside.

A few minutes later they had a table in the shade. While they waited for the drinks she'd ordered, she pulled out the cars. "You can play with your new toys while we wait."

The two boys were soon making rumbling sounds as they zoomed the cars around on the table. She watched

them, already knowing who was who. Juan was definitely more outgoing and courageous. Pablo was more timid and quiet. Alike in looks, they were totally different in personality.

"Finished shopping already?" Luis asked from behind her. Stacey turned and smiled. "Just taking a break."

"Look at our new toys, Daddy," Pablo said, holding up his car. "We saw the man make a bird."

Luis pulled out the fourth chair and sat with them. "Nice cars. I'd like to see a man make a bird."

Stacey pulled out her humming bird and Luis reached for it, brushing his fingers against hers as she took it. She felt the touch to her toes. Had he done it deliberately? Sitting back in her chair, she wished she could put more distance between them. A good night's sleep and she was still feeling more aware of her employer than ever before. Not that he wasn't handsome as all get-out, even though not the dark Spaniard she'd expected.

He glanced at her and smiled as he handed the bird back. Her heart skipped a beat and then raced. Good grief, she had to clamp down on those fantasies that were starting to swirl. He was her boss for three weeks, the father of her charges. Nothing more.

She repeated the mantra over and over as she re-wrapped the bird and put it back in the bag.

"Did you say something?" Luis asked.

Shaking her head, Stacey was very grateful when the waiter arrived with her *café con leche* and the boys' lemonade. Luis quickly ordered coffee.

"Finished your work?" she asked.

"They limit the time on the computers. There's quite a line. More computers would increase their business," he said.

"Maybe the owners like it the way it is," she suggested.

When his coffee was delivered, he asked the boys what they liked best about the market. Learning they had not yet seen the fish stalls, he offered to show them that after they finished their snack. "It was always my favorite as a young kid. Once a teenager, anything to do with the market was strictly not cool."

He glanced at the boys and looked away.

Spotting his suddenly sad look, Stacey began to wonder what he thought about when he looked at them.

"Do the twins resemble their mother?" She didn't think so, but she'd never seen a photo of Melissa. To her they looked like a blond version of their father.

"Every time I look at them, I see her. She never even got to hold them, she died during delivery."

"I'm so sorry," she said softly.

The boys were in their own world, racing their cars across the table.

"What a joy that you see her every day in their sweet faces."

"No joy, only regret at the way things turned out."

"Oh, you should be happy to see her. A tangible legacy she left behind."

He looked at her for a moment, obviously turning over the words in his mind. "I never thought about it that way, only how hard it is to look at them and not wish she was still with us."

"That will probably never completely go away, but in the meantime you owe it to her to spend time with your sons. She would want that, surely?" Again she was butting in where she shouldn't. But she was growing to care for her charges and knew they'd enjoy the summer more spending more time with their father.

"Why do I get the feeling you're in collusion with my grandmother, trying to wean me away from work altogether?" he asked.

She laughed. "Not so. But it is a vacation. Surely you've hired smart men and women to work with you at the firm. Can't they manage without you for a few days?"

"Twenty-one days is almost a month," he retorted.

She tilted her head, watching him.

"And, yes, I do have competent employees." He glanced at the boys. "Okay, between you and my grandmother, and the short time at the internet café, I give up. From now on this vacation will be about the boys. Any work needed to be done will be after they're asleep in the evenings. Which works out better for timing in the US anyway."

"Good move." She felt audacious telling him how to spend his vacation, but happy for the boys' sake that their dad would spend more time with them.

"Okay, boys, ready to have your dad show you the fish booths? I can't wait."

"Me, too," Juan and Pablo said in unison.

Walking through the crowd down a wide aisle they had not yet covered, Stacey held Pablo's hand while Luis held Juan's. Walking side by side, the boys between them, she was struck again by their resemblance to a family.

Why was she harping on that? Was it her recent thoughts about settling down? Or wishful thinking, with Luis taking the starring role? She'd asked quietly when they prepared to leave the café if he wanted them to himself, but Luis quickly said he wanted her part of the group. The offhand comment had warmed her beyond what was intended, she was sure.

The next hour passed swiftly as Luis showed the boys the fish stalls, which they thoroughly enjoyed, even hold-

ing some of the fish, much to Stacey's dismay. They'd smell all the way home! She said nothing, however, enjoying their delight in the activity and watching as they seemed to blossom with their dad's attention.

Finally Luis checked his watch. "Lunch will be served at Abuela Maria's soon. We better get back or I'll get scolded for being late."

Juan thought that was hilarious and he asked if his father was often scolded.

"More so when I was your age. Gradually I realized it was easier to follow the rules. In fact, sometimes I even got a treat for following the rules," Luis said, with the briefest hint of smile.

"Like what?" Pablo asked.

Stacey wanted the answer to that as well. Might help with future dealings with his children

"Extra cake after dinner, or being allowed to stay up late for fiesta."

"What's fiesta?" Juan asked.

"Ah, lots of fun. Though I haven't been in years, there'll be a fiesta here in a couple of weeks. We'll plan to go—if you two are good and take a nap that day. You'll want to stay up for the fireworks."

"Is it Fourth of July?" Pablo asked, fascinated at the thought of staying up late.

"No, but celebrated almost as much." He looked at Stacey. "You'll have to come, too. It's the festival of one of the saints and as much fun as the Fourth is at home."

She nodded, wondering what his grandmother would say. Wasn't fiesta a time for families to celebrate? Would they really want her to tag along?

When they arrived back at the villa, she whisked the boys upstairs for a quick wash to clean up for lunch. She would have liked more time alone with just Luis and the

boys, but knew her job wasn't to entertain her boss but to watch his children.

When they returned to the terrace, the main table had been extended and numerous chairs surrounded it. The smaller table by the flowers had also been stretched and the chairs expanded to half a dozen.

There were already several people talking, gesturing and laughing.

Pablo leaned against Stacey, his eyes wide and apprehensive as he surveyed the strangers.

Luis gestured them over.

"Here we go. More cousins, I bet," Stacey whispered, urging the boys to the group.

A flurry of introductions was made. Luis's cousins Sebastian and his wife and children, his cousin Theresa, her husband and daughter were all introduced. Stacey was surprised when Luis introduced her that he made no mention she was the boys' nanny. Stacey had a hard time nailing down all the names. She knew the twins wouldn't have a chance. Juan was happy to talk to the other children, each of whom seemed to speak rudimentary English, but Pablo clung to Stacey. She put her arm around his shoulders and hugged him gently. Leaning over, she whispered, "It'll get easier once we sort out all the names to faces. Maybe everyone should wear name badges."

Pablo looked up at her. "I can't read very well."

"I'd read them all for you. But we'll get to know these people and then you'll forget you ever didn't know their names. The two boys are a bit older than you, but I think your cousin Alli is about your age."

He nodded and looked at the little girl who looked almost as shy as he was.

Stacey took his hand and went to her.

"This is Pablo. Do you speak English?" Stacey said in Spanish.

She shook her head, watching warily.

"Unfortunately he doesn't speak Spanish, but perhaps I can translate for you two. Shall we eat together at the small table?"

"*Sí, por favor.* There are so many grown-ups. We always eat at the kids' table. It's more fun."

Stacey translated for Pablo, then held out her hand for Alli to take. In less than five minutes all the children were at the small table, Stacey sitting at the head, rapidly translating back and forth.

Maria stopped by before she went to the main table. "I didn't mean for you to be stuck with the children. Please join us."

"*Gracias*, Senora, but I think it best for now to translate between them. If they finish early, may they be excused to go to the playroom?"

"*Sí*, but only if you come and join the rest of the adults."

"I'm the boys' nanny," Stacey reminded her.

"But you deserve some grown-up time as well. After they eat. Do join us."

Stacey recognized a directive when she heard one. She smiled and nodded.

Turning her attention back to the children, she also kept an eye on the adult table—especially on Luis. For the first time he seemed relaxed and enjoying himself. He laughed when something was said and she looked away quickly. She needed to focus on the children, not her handsome employer.

When everyone at her table finished she asked if they wanted to go to the playroom. Amidst the cheers

of agreement, Pablo looked at her. "Are you coming, too?"

"I'm going to stay down here with the adults for a little while. I'll come up when lunch is over."

"But I can't understand them. What if they talk to me and I can't answer?" he asked, his eyes wide with worry.

"Juan will be with you, so someone will speak English. And Pedro speaks a little English, he can translate if needed. And if you play with cars, you'll all have the same ideas, I bet. " Her heart ached for the little boy. This vacation was a lot to take in for him.

"Come with me. We'll play together if we can't speak with the others," Juan said. "We can explore the playroom."

The children left the terrace and Stacey rose and went to join the other adults. The only empty chair was beside Luis. She refused to read anything into that as she slid in next to him. Grateful for the years of Spanish study, she had little difficulty understanding everyone, though they spoke more rapidly than she did. Once or twice when she said something, Sebastian laughed.

"Am I saying it wrong?" she asked.

"Not wrong, but different," Luis explained. "Mexican influence, I expect."

That led the conversation into how she'd learned and where. Sebastian's wife Anna then said, "I'm learning English. I never have chance to practice. Maybe you and I…?"

"Sure, and you can correct my Spanish," Stacey said.

The conversation veered to family matters and Stacey listened enthralled. The extended Aldivista family sounded wonderful to her. There was only her sister left of her family. Their grandmother had died when Savannah had been in college. She'd been elderly and in

frail health as long as Stacey had known her. Sometimes she wondered if she'd held on to life until she'd seen her granddaughters firmly launched into their own lives.

They had no family home. The modest cabin they'd grown up in was nothing in comparison to this villa and it had been sold to pay the final expenses and finish Savannah's education after Grams had died.

Luis placed his arm across the back of her chair. She kept her gaze from him but was very tempted to lean back enough to touch. Once she glanced at Maria and found the older woman studying her grandson, her glance flicking to Stacey.

Oh, my, Stacey thought. Was she now regretting her invitation? Surely she didn't think she was interested in Luis. A dynamic man like Luis didn't stay single for six years just to fall for a temporary nanny.

After lunch, several of the adults went to take a siesta. Stacey went to get the boys and take them swimming. Pedro, Paloma and Alli, the younger cousins, all wanted to go as well. Anna decided to accompany Stacey. Luis disappeared and she wondered if he was going back to the internet café. So much for spending time with his boys.

The afternoon was fun and the twins grew more comfortable around the other three cousins. Pedro as the oldest had a tendency to be bossy, but none of the others cared. Anna and Stacey swam, watched, refereed, and sat under an umbrella and talked in English.

Dinner was at seven. Once again they ate on the veranda, the children at one table, the adults at the bigger one. This time Maria insisted Stacey join them at the beginning of the meal. The conversation was lively as everyone caught up on the past few months and years. Stacey enjoyed learning more about Luis's family. She'd

have an easier time remembering who was who and what they did.

When they were finished, Maria said, "We made plans for tomorrow. I thought during the day you and your families can play on the beach. Tomorrow night we've been invited to Mario Sabata's for dinner." She looked at Stacey. "Mario is an old friend of my husband's. His house is about a half-hour drive up in the hills, with a lovely view of the sea. Do join us. I'll have one of the maids watch the children."

"Oh, but that's my job," Stacey said with a glance at Luis. He removed his arm from her chair.

"If you'd like to join us, please do. Mario has many fine antiques you might like to see," he said stiffly, with a hard glance at his grandmother.

"But we don't take the children. We were, what, in our teens before we were allowed to visit," Sebastian said. "Mario's a bit picky about who comes to his house. He wants no damage, you understand."

"And one can never expect children to be perfect. He's become more fussy with age. But he raised three daughters, he and his wife," Maria said. "At least you had manners by the time you first went. It'll be an enjoyable evening, I'm sure. If we are all finished with dinner, I'd prefer a more comfortable chair in the lounge."

Dinner was officially over. Stacey hung back as everyone filed into the house. Bringing up the rear, she followed as far as the stairs and then took them to go check on the boys. Reaching the playroom, she paused in the doorway to watch a moment. All five children were playing together. The mishmash of words showed the twins were picking up Spanish at a good rate. And from a couple of words Alli said, she was starting to pick up English too.

Pablo spotted her first. "Stacey, I'm glad you're here." He rushed over and gave her a hug.

She hugged him back. "Having fun?"

"I still can't understand them but we're playing cars and having races and one time mine won!"

"Fabulous. Can I watch?"

"Yes." He took her hand and led her over to the others. Stacey sat down on the floor ready to be entertained by the children. They had a fresh perspective on life, which she enjoyed seeing. Occasionally she translated back and forth, but was pleased to see they were managing fine among themselves.

Some time later, the twins in bed, read to and left to sleep, she went back to her room. The evening was still early enough to enjoy. Opening her French doors, she stepped out onto the wide balcony. It faced the garden with the sea to the right. Walking to the corner, she leaned against the post. The illumination was faint, but enough to see by. She could hear the murmur of the waves along the shore, smell the fragrance of the flowers perfuming the air. It was balmy, breezy and delightful.

"I think my grandmother expected you in the salon as well," Luis said behind her.

Stacey turned, leaning against the railing. She could just make out his silhouette in the starlight. Had he planned to retire and found her on the balcony that encircled the house?

"She was kind enough to include me at dinner. I didn't want to push my luck. My job's to watch the twins. I was worried about Pablo and the language barrier."

He stepped closer, looking out toward the dark expanse that was the Mediterranean. "How are they faring?"

"Doing well. We played a word game in English and Spanish, which all the children seemed to enjoy. I think Alli especially likes being with your boys. The other two are older. Are yours not around other children much?"

"Just at school and when Hannah takes them to the park. Otherwise I guess not. She doesn't encourage play dates."

Stacey nodded. "I wondered. They play well together with others, but seem to hold back a little."

"When the rest of the family arrives, there'll be even more kids. Is it too much for them? Maybe we should have stayed in a hotel."

"They'll have the summer of their lives," Stacey said. "Tomorrow we're planning a castle-building contest on the beach. Do you know I never even saw a beach until I was eighteen?"

"Really? You never went on vacation to the shore?"

"Never. My grandmother had arthritis and it was too painful for her to do much. And we didn't have the money. After my first visit, I was hooked. I'd build a house by the sea if I could and live there forever."

"Until then you take other people's children to the shore?"

"What better way to see all the oceans in the world and decide the best one for me when I settle down?"

"And what's your favorite so far?"

"I haven't seen them all yet. Mostly the Caribbean and the Pacific. I'd like to visit the Seychelles, Australia, even see all the Great Lakes, they have beaches just like the oceans. But most of my trips are to exotic locales. I probably will just buy a home by the sea in Maryland when I retire and watch the Atlantic all day long."

"I can't see you sitting all day long," he said.

"Some days it holds a lot of appeal. Not that I'm complaining. I'm glad to enjoy children while I can."

"Until you have your own?"

She shrugged. "Until then."

"So no hopes of marriage soon?"

She laughed softly. "Hardly. It's difficult to meet eligible bachelors when I travel so much. There is Phillip. He lives in our building, but he's a starving artist. I left that kind of life behind. I choose to have a bit more money in the bank and in exchange for watching children, which I love doing, I get to travel the world on someone else's dime. How cool is that?"

"Except I expect living vicariously through other families isn't as satisfying as it might seem," he said after a moment.

Stacey looked at him, wishing she could see him better.

"I still get a thrill when I find out where my next assignment will be." Which was true. Only lately the thrill wasn't as big as it once had been. More and more she felt a tug of reluctance to take off again. She began to want to make a home, become part of a community. Have more friends that she could see whenever she wanted and not only between travels.

"I get a lot of satisfaction from my work. If I didn't, I'd get out and do something else. When the job palls, what will you do?" he asked.

"Maybe I'll take over the office part of Vacation Nannies. Traveling is fun, but as I approach a milestone birthday, I'm reassessing what I want."

"Milestone birthday? Let me guess, thirty?"

She nodded. "I got my education, have traveled the world. Now I think it's time for more reflection and a different plan for the rest of my life."

"Life has a way of knocking plans cockeyed," he said.

"True. Then I'd just make new plans. Look at you, did you ever envision the success you'd have when you were twenty?"

"No. But success isn't a guarantee. Neither, once having achieved it, is staying on top assured."

"I know. I also believe people should do what they love. However, being the boss has certain perks. You can structure your hours however you like."

"Within limits, you're right."

Dared she ask why then he chose to work when his young children were awake and not wait until they were in school or asleep? Stacey kept quiet. It wasn't her place to tell parents how to raise their children. In three weeks this assignment would end and she'd likely never come in contact with Luis Aldivista or his twins again.

The silence seemed comfortable, Stacey thought. She didn't feel she needed to rush into speech to fill a void.

"This is nice," she said after another moment passed. "And a lovely place for the boys to spend a few weeks. I think by the end of our stay they'll know all their relatives and speak a bit of Spanish to boot."

"My folks will be here soon. They see them each year."

"You're lucky. Your boys are lucky," she said softly.

"How so?"

"My sister and I are all that's our family. Everyone else is gone. You have so much family, wonderful stories about growing up, spending summers together. A nice legacy for your boys."

"Doesn't make up for them not having a mother."

"Of course not. But I know what's important when parents die. Spending time with those who knew them. Grams used to tell us all about our mother, when she was

young, when she started dating, how she met our dad. You can do that. Tell them about when you were growing up. Talk to them about their mother. I was six when mine died, so I have few memories. Savannah, my sister, was younger, so doesn't have any. Juan and Pablo have no memories of their mother so they need to get to know her through you and her family."

"Melissa's parents live in Florida. They rarely see the boys." He was quiet for a moment. "They didn't approve of our marriage."

"Why ever not?" That surprised Stacey. She'd consider it an amazing miracle if a man like Luis ever wanted to marry her.

"At the time I was like your struggling artist friend, not a dime to my name. We worked hard together. Yet she never got to enjoy the fruit of that."

"I bet you both were happy to work together and plan for the future. She must have been thrilled to be expecting twins."

"Yes. And we had just reached the point where she could stay at home with them. That was the plan."

She didn't want to talk about his dead wife. She knew he must have loved her extravagantly to still be mourning her loss six years later.

"I'm off to bed now. Busy day tomorrow." She started back to her room then paused and turned.

"Should I really be going to your grandmother's friends tomorrow night? I feel awkward. I was hired to watch the twins, not socialize with your family."

"As long as you realize her invitation is one of graciousness and not some matchmaking scheme that doesn't have any basis in reality, feel free to acquiesce to her bidding. We'll enjoy the vacation, return home and go our separate ways."

Wow, so much for wishful thinking. Luis was cynical and definitely not interested in pursuing any kind of friendship with her.

"Trust me, Mr. Aldivista. The thought never entered my mind." More than a dozen times, she finished silently. "I'll make sure I keep my distance."

"Goodnight, Stacey. Perhaps it was my lucky day when I called Vacation Nannies."

Stacey was glad he thought so. She had major doubts and this evening a few of those had popped into mind. Mainly because she coveted his family. They were warm, friendly, connected. She could envision family gatherings every summer, seeing how all the children grew, keeping in touch with cousins and the older generation during the year. Exchanging photographs and letters, video communications.

Fantasy thinking. Which Luis had just made perfectly clear he did not share.

She and Savannah would establish their own homes and families one of these days. And it wouldn't include the man she'd turned her back on.

Luis watched as Stacey walked to her room and entered, leaving the French doors open for the night breeze. She was unlike anyone he knew, yet he'd been amazed at how quickly the boys had accepted her. Pablo quicker than ever expected. And in only the two days she'd been on board, their behavior had improved. What was her secret?

Luis turned and leaned against the railing, gazing out toward the sea. When the moon rose, it would be illuminated, but for now the few stars out didn't offer enough light. He took a deep breath, loving the tangy scent of salt in the air, mixing with the fragrance of the garden.

Closing his eyes for a moment, he was taken back to childhood days. Teen years, slipping out of the house at night for a forbidden swim or to attend to the festival. Years before life had intruded with all its foibles.

Years before he'd met Melissa, fallen in love and started life with her. Then the beginnings of the company, her death, and life as he now knew it.

He had a yearning to slip back to those carefree teen years, when the worst he'd had to deal with had been his grandparents finding his stash of firecrackers to be used during fiesta.

Melissa had not liked her visit here. The language barrier had presented a definite problem and she had complained about not liking the food, about the constant company of family. They had only made the one visit. And after she'd died, it had been impossible to recapture the optimism he'd once enjoyed. He felt the weight of the world sometimes. Responsible for his sons. For the firm where so many depended on him to keep it growing.

Stacey was as different from Melissa as night was from day. She seemed to relish the conversation tonight at the dinner table, laughing, asking questions about people, getting a brief bio on many of the family.

His *abuela* seemed taken with her. Surprising for such a short acquaintance. Usually Abuela Maria stood on more formal ceremony. She was loving to her family, but more reserved with new acquaintances. More kudos to Stacey. She'd charmed his children and his grandmother.

He smiled, thinking about her laughter at one of the escapades Sebastian had related—with *he* the miscreant in the scenario. Once or twice during the evening he'd seen his cousins exchange glances. It wasn't as if he was looking to marry again. He'd loved his wife and he couldn't imagine falling for another woman like that. Or

letting himself be a hostage to fate a second time. What if he married again and that wife died? A man could only take so much.

Still, if he ever considered marriage again, he'd want someone who loved his sons, and whom the twins loved in return. Someone young and sophisticated, an asset to assist in building the company. When the image of Stacey popped into mind, he scowled in disgust. He was not going there. Standing, he hit the railing lightly with a fist. If he were to remarry, he'd find his own wife, not be enticed by a pretty blonde who made him laugh.

He considered how he could spend more time with the boys. He wanted them to have as happy memories of visiting Spain as he did. To remember their childhood with warmth, not just think of their father on vacation.

Hadn't he bemoaned that very fact when he'd been younger? His father had traveled extensively—the primary reason he and Isabella had been sent to their grandparents' place each summer. During the year Luis remembered more about his father asking him how his schoolwork was going than anything else.

Had he ever played ball with his son? Even holidays had centered around his father's work. For a moment Luis paused, gripping the rail tightly. He was turning into his father. And he hated the notion.

He refused to become like that. Many of the employees in the company already telecommuted to work. With the electronic age, he could do the same. Conference calls were already handled electronically. Instant messaging would give even more immediate access than finding a time to sit down face-to-face.

A lot of what he did didn't even require interaction with others. His first love was programming. He became more intrigued with the thought as he considered

how he could implement such a radical change. At the office early in the morning, home with the boys in the afternoons, work on programming after the twins went to bed. It could be done.

Turning, he headed back to his dark bedroom. Pausing at the open French doors, he listened to see if he could hear Stacey. Her room was also dark. Had she gone to bed like she'd said?

Giving in to impulse, he went through his room to the hall, then upstairs to check on his sons. They slept peacefully. Looking at them, Luis felt a wave of love.

He'd start tomorrow. Internet café in the morning, time with the boys in the afternoon, grandmother's excursion in the evening.

He'd enlist Stacey in his plans and see how much they could accomplish before returning to New York.

Return home and bid Stacey goodbye. He turned, not wanting to think that far ahead.

CHAPTER FOUR

STACEY and the boys spent the morning with the other children and their parents at the beach. The sun shone in a cloudless sky. Stacey also made sure the twins had a rest from playing and swimming every hour, offering them bottled water that Abuela Maria made sure each one took to the beach. The kids swam, built sandcastles, played water games and would have been as wrinkled as little prunes had they not been called out of the water periodically.

Stacey kept a close eye on the boys, though she sat with Sebastian's wife Anna beneath the shade of the umbrella. Anna was pleased she had someone to sit with as Sebastian had gone off with Luis right after breakfast.

"You have not known the family long," Anna said in her halting English..

"No, I only met them a few days ago." Was it only four days ago?

"Tell me about Vacation Nannies. An unusual concept, I believe," Anna said.

"A lot of fun, too. I love children, and I love to travel even more. This job offers both."

"Hard to fit in with a family with such short times together, I'd think," Anna said, watching the children play in the sea.

"Not as difficult as you might believe. Everyone knows it's just temporary. Parents like it because it gives them a trustworthy babysitter when they wish to go out. The kids have the same person watching them the entire trip. And there's no language problem when visiting a foreign country. For instance, if Luis had come alone with the boys, he'd have to find someone around here available for a couple of weeks who also spoke English."

"If he had come. This is his first visit with the boys, you know," Anna said. "He came once before they were born, with his wife. She didn't like it here."

"Because of the language barrier?" Stacey asked.

"That and other things. It was a tragic shock when she died. She appeared to be in perfect health the one time I met her."

"Luis still misses her," Stacey murmured.

"Hmm, I'm sure he does, but the early pangs of grief have long faded. Work consumes him now, if what Sebastian says is true. He should get married again and have more children. He's still a young man, with decades ahead of him. How sad to spend it alone."

"He has the twins," Stacey reminded her, smiling at the antics of the boys at the water's edge. They were fast becoming her favorite charges ever.

"Um, not the same. But men will do what they wish. Tell me about life in America. We might go visit when the children are a little older."

Stacey described her apartment and how she and her sister juggled their jobs and still found time to spend together. The morning passed swiftly and before she knew it they were rounding up the children to head back for lunch pleasantly tired from races, swimming underwater and each trying to outdo the others.

Everyone went back to the villa to shower and dress

for lunch. Stacey was amazed at how quickly Juan and Pablo were learning basic Spanish. With the other children not speaking much English, they had to in order to communicate. She was readily available to translate, but was required to do so less and less.

When she stepped out onto the veranda, Maria gestured her over. "I believe the children can manage their meals on their own for now. Please join us."

Stacey didn't know how to refuse without being rude, so she gave in and sat where she'd sat the previous night.

Luis and Sebastian arrived before everyone had been seated, avoiding a scolding for being late, Stacey thought, amused by the comment he'd made yesterday.

"Successful morning?" she asked quietly as he sat beside her.

"Caught up on some things. Everyone's doing okay. I even received an email from Hannah for the boys. She hopes they're having fun, which," he said, looking over at the children's table, "they appear to be doing."

"We had a great time on the beach this morning. They are going to be excellent swimmers by the end of the vacation."

Theresa and her husband announced they'd just learned she was pregnant and wanted to share the good news with the family. Excited congratulations were given and the conversation turned to family names. Stacey loved listening. By the end of the week even more relatives would arrive and the house and guest house would be bursting. She could tell by the sparkle in Maria's eyes how much she loved having everyone gather. Her birthday was actually the following week, but she wanted a long celebration, she explained.

After lunch, Stacey had the boys lie down for a short rest. They fell asleep almost instantly, tired from their

morning's activities. She was just tiptoeing from their room when Luis showed up.

"Are they asleep?" he asked.

"For a little while. They played hard this morning. And you'll be pleased to see how much Spanish they're learning. Pablo surprised me by learning more and his accent is quite good. Juan rushes everything, but he's learning, too. By the end of the visit I bet they don't need help translating at all."

"I've heard that kids learn fast."

"Especially when that's pretty much all they're going to hear while we're here. Except from you and me, and maybe we should speak Spanish first and then English."

"Immersion works, I've been told. So now what?"

"What do you mean?"

"I had planned to spend the afternoon with them, but if they're going to sleep it away, I'm at a loose end."

Stacey laughed softly. "I doubt that. Visit with your grandmother?" she suggested.

"Apparently she had a busy morning as well and has gone for a short siesta. As has everyone else. I never acquired that habit. Come with me to the beach. You're probably tired of it, but I'd love a swim."

"I never tire of the beach. And watching children learn to swim isn't the same as swimming myself." She gave it three seconds of thought—then threw caution to the wind. "I'll change and meet you on the terrace," she said. She knew he had to be bored, with everyone else in their rooms, but she couldn't help the small thrill of anticipation that rose, thinking about swimming together. He could have gone off by himself.

The water was cool but not cold when they waded out until it became deep enough to dive beneath the surface.

Luis was a strong swimmer and Stacey was hard pressed to keep up with him. They swam for several minutes before he stopped and began to tread water.

The Med was especially buoyant so it took little effort to keep upright.

She tipped her head back to have the water pull her hair from her face. She could tell by the refraction of the light that droplets clung to her eyelashes.

"This is perfect," she said, turning to look at the shore. The villa rose behind where they'd dropped their towels, caressed by the trees and shrubbery. The garden couldn't be seen from this vantage point as it was hidden by the shrubs.

"I'm starting to feel like I'm on vacation. The rest of the day is free," Luis said, studying Stacey. He didn't want to be drawn to her but, despite his best attempts, he'd thought about her while waiting for different responses from emails he'd sent.

She never crossed the line between employee and employer. No flirting. It was refreshing. Sometimes he felt like the women he knew in New York only saw him in dollar signs. Granted, he'd made enough to live in any manner he wished. What others didn't seem to realize was that he was content with his lifestyle. It was safer than having his heart held hostage to fate. He only had his boys to worry about. They were young and healthy.

"Race you back," Stacey said, and began swimming furiously toward shore.

Luis waited a moment, then began to follow her, passing her long before they reached the sand.

He stood in the shallows and waited until she caught up.

"I win. What's the prize?" he asked.

She stood, wringing water from her hair, grinning up

at him. He felt that stab of awareness again. She looked young and carefree and happy. Involuntarily, he grinned back.

"I'll let you read the bedtime story to the boys," she said.

"A nice enough treat, but not very special."

"Then what would you suggest?" she said, walking slowly toward their towels.

A kiss popped into mind.

The idea startled him and his smile faded. He was not going there. First of all, it would be totally inappropriate. Second, he wasn't getting entangled with anyone. He liked his life the way it was.

She glanced over her shoulder at him, her eyes sparkling with mischief. "I know, your sons and I will serve you breakfast in bed tomorrow."

"Ah, who could refuse that?" He debated following her to the chaises beneath the umbrella but needed distance.

"I'm going back out." With that he turned and swam as hard as he could to chase away the image of Stacey in his arms, her warm, wet skin against his, only their bathing suits separating them. The image was hard to dispel, until he swam harder, pushing himself to forget all about those disturbing images. A lesson learned. Do not be alone with Stacey in the future.

When he started back some time later he saw she was no longer on the beach. Better that way. He took his time and was pleasantly tired when he scooped up his towel. The twins might be awake by now. He'd change and see. Maybe he'd give the nanny the rest of the afternoon off to get ready for the dinner party, and take his sons with Sebastian and explore further along the beach.

* * *

Stacey was ready at the time appointed by Maria to leave for dinner. She always traveled with one little black dress and strappy sandals, which took up no room. Her hair looked lighter from her time in the sun and curled naturally. She pulled it back from her face, but let it hang down her back. Grabbing a small purse, she went to check on the boys. One of the maids was giving them dinner and would put all the children to bed. The five children were on the terrace, already eating and laughing.

"Stacey, you look very pretty," Pablo said when he saw her. He left the table and ran over to her. "Why can't I come?"

"This is for grown-ups only, sweetie. Another time maybe your dad will take you out for dinner." She leaned over and whispered in his ear, "Be good and go to bed right when you're told, all right?"

"Okay." He reached up to hug her as Luis came out onto the terrace. Stacey hugged Pablo and then Juan when he ran over.

"Be good, okay?" she said.

"*Sí*," Juan said.

Pablo nodded solemnly.

After bidding his sons goodnight, Luis turned to Stacey. "Ready? Grandmother is in the foyer with the others. We'll take two cars. I volunteered to drive the one I rented. Sebastian and Anna will ride with us. Grandmother will have her driver take the others."

"Fine. I'm ready." She was conscious of how amazing Luis looked in his dark suit, snowy white shirt and dark blue tie. Her heart kicked into higher gear when his hand touched the small of her back as they entered the house. Suddenly she questioned what she was doing, going out with the family. Her place was really with the children.

"How lovely you look," Theresa said when they joined

the others in the foyer. She was wearing a ruby-red dress that went well with her dark coloring.

Stacey was relieved to know her dress fit in. She hoped there wouldn't be other excursions as she only had the one dressy dress.

Luis followed his grandmother's driver to a house high in the hills that overlooked the sea. The home was glowing in the late afternoon sun, the sandy-colored walls enhanced by the terracotta roof and dark brown trim. Large windows faced the sea, affording magnificent views in all directions. The windows were open for the breeze, light curtains billowing.

"Mario has lived here his entire life, I think," Sebastian said as he helped Anna from the back of the car.

When she got out of the car, Stacey turned to look at the view. A sweeping vista of the village below and the sea as far as she could see. In the distance a large ship was moving west.

"Pretty, isn't it?" Anna said as she passed Stacey and headed for the house. Stacey nodded and turned to enter the large home.

Their host looked to be in his late fifties. He and Maria were obviously long-time friends. His younger daughter Pilar served as hostess. Cocktails were served on the terrace that overlooked the sea. Dinner was in the formal dining room.

To Stacey's surprise, she was not seated next to Luis. Feeling a bit foolish, thinking this had been a ploy to push them together, she was glad no one could read minds. Maybe she'd read things entirely wrong, or maybe she'd hoped for more. She did little talking, content to listen as others discussed mutual friends, and events coming with the fiesta.

After dinner, they moved to the salon, where Pilar gave in to entreaties to play the piano. She was a pianist of concert quality, Stacey decided soon after she began to play. The music was lovely. Some classical, some modern and one flamenco that had her foot tapping and her wishing she could do the dance that was so popular in the south of Spain.

Stacey smiled at Maria, sitting next to her on one sofa. "She has a marvelous talent," she said.

"She's studied for many years," Maria said. "She brings a lot of joy with the music. Do you play an instrument?"

"No." There had been no extra money for frivolities like music when she'd been growing up. She could sing passably well, but that was the extent of her musical abilities.

"Sadly neither do any of my children or grandchildren. Perhaps there is hope for the next generation. I shall speak to Luis and suggest he have his sons learn something. Even if it's not a career, playing can bring happiness."

"One of the children I watched a few months ago plays the violin, and she's only nine. She begged to be allowed to learn when she was six and proved an accomplished violinist almost from the first lesson. Most children don't start that young."

"It takes a commitment on the part of the student as well as the parents," Maria said, watching as Pilar rose and went to join Luis, Sebastian and her father who had begun to talk after she'd finished her last piece.

"Um," Maria said, studying her grandson and Pilar. "Do you think Luis will marry again?" she asked.

"Goodness, I just met him a few days ago. I have no idea," Stacey said, also looking over at the group. Pilar

laughed at something Luis said and Stacey was struck by how lovely she was. Her dark hair flowed around her shoulders. Her brown eyes looked merry when she smiled. She had to be a few years older than Luis, but they had a lot in common.

"I worry about him. He and his wife were happy. Though she didn't like Spain. Still, a small price to pay for a grandson's happiness."

"Maybe he'd return here to live if he were to marry a Spanish woman," Stacey said. For a moment she felt a pang. What if he was captivated by Pilar and spent the rest of the vacation courting her?

It would change nothing. She was here to watch the boys and she hardly knew him really. Forcing herself to look away, she glanced through the open French doors to the terrace. "Would you care to go with me on the terrace to see the village lights?" Stacey asked. She did not want to discuss family matters with her employer's grandmother. She didn't even want to think beyond this evening.

"I have seen it many times. Go. I will join my friend Mario and see what the lively discussion is about."

Stacey nodded and crossed the room to the terrace. There was a stone wall around the perimeter she went to perch on. The moon had not yet risen, though there was plenty of light on the terrace from the salon. Below her the village glittered. The view was as pretty now as in daylight.

"Admiring Alta Parisa by night?" Luis asked a moment later.

Stacey looked back to where he stood near the door and nodded. "It's so pleasant and peaceful here and the village fairly sparkles. Señor Sabata has a lovely home."

"But I'm betting you'd prefer to be closer to the water," he said, walking across to join her.

"You're right. I love being able to step off the villa's pathway right onto the beach. Here one would have to drive several minutes to get to the beach."

"Not to mention it would be a public beach, more crowded than the space in front of Abuela's villa."

"Mmm."

Luis stared out at the view. It had been a long time since he'd enjoyed an evening so much. The conversation had not centered on work. Catching up with what Mario and Pilar had been doing reminded him how often he'd seen them when he'd been younger. Both Mario's and Abuela's spouses were dead now, but at one time both families had spent a lot of time together. Pilar had lorded it over him and Isabel as she was several years older. Still, the memories were happy for the most part. And it was good to catch up on her life now.

He glanced at Stacey, who seemed content to gaze out into the night and enjoy the lights of the village. She was easy to be with, never made any demands, never seemed to expect more than she was given. What made her tick?

He was fascinated by her and wanted to learn more. May as well, they'd be sharing this vacation for another two weeks. Apparently he'd been wrong about his grandmother's motives in placing Stacey in the room next to his. Tonight would have been the perfect opportunity to seat them side by side; instead, he'd been at the other end of the table from Stacey.

He placed one foot on the wall and listened idly to the soft murmur of the conversations in the salon. Bringing the boys this summer gave him a chance to reconnect with people he'd known growing up, and give Juan and

Pablo memories of a lifestyle different from theirs in New York.

"Did you come here often when you spent your summers in Alta Parisa?" Stacey asked.

"Enough for Pilar to be the bossy older sister neither Isabel nor I wanted. But she's a part of the past and has improved with age."

Stacey laughed. He liked listening to her laughter. She seemed happier than any other person he knew.

"Maybe it's you who changed," she suggested.

"I was perfect from the beginning," he responded.

She laughed again. "Just like your twins."

"Not even I as their father can call them perfect. But I can see the change already. You're good for them."

"Sometimes Juan can be a bit stubborn or cantankerous."

"You can't blame anything like that on Pablo," he said, remembering some of the trouble they'd caused last fall when he'd taken them shopping one Saturday afternoon. "But they can be wild and hard to handle. You seem to have the knack."

"They're well-adjusted little boys, full of life and seeking adventure. You should join them on the beach tomorrow and see how their swimming's improving. They tried underwater today, encouraged by their cousins."

"If they're going to nap every day, I might switch my time at the internet café and spend mornings with them."

"They would love that. I can't guarantee they'll nap every day. Both told me they are too old. But today they were so tired they were asleep before I finished the story book."

"They like you," Luis said.

"That's good. I hope all my kids like me. It makes the vacation so much more fun."

"Have you had any children not like you?"

"Once in a great while. Mostly because they're rebelling against their parents. When they reach a certain age, they're convinced they need no one to watch them, but are truly too young to be alone in a foreign country. I prefer younger children. My sister, on the other hand, specialized in adolescent behavior, and loves the challenges of teens."

"Tell me about the worst job you ever had," he said.

Stacey thought a moment then nodded. "The Jones brats. No other word for them." She proceeded to tell Luis about the teenagers who had tried the entire vacation to escape her watchful eye. He could picture the two girls pulling the pranks as she described them.

When she finished, he said, "Yet, despite all that, you speak about them with affection."

"I haven't met a kid yet whom I don't like. Some have not had a very good raising. Others are just pushing boundaries, trying to find their way. But everyone has some redeeming qualities. I look for those."

"Don't you get tired of constant travel? I thought women were nesters. Why don't you have a home of your own, kids of your own?"

"Maybe someday." She was silent so long Luis didn't think she was going to speak again and was about to suggest they return inside as it was growing cooler in the evening breeze. Her comments caught him by surprise.

"My sister and I didn't have a lot growing up. We always longed to travel. Perhaps if we'd gone on some vacation trips as kids that longing would have been satisfied. Instead, it built and built. We were really poor, too poor to go anywhere. Sometimes we lived on just potatoes and rice until grandmother got her monthly check. It's hard to grow up without so much that other children

take for granted—like bicycles. Neither Savannah nor I ever had a bike as a kid, yet most of the kids we went to school with did. That kind of thing can set you apart. So I decided when I was old enough to figure things out that I wanted nice things, I wanted to travel and see the world.."

"But the right man would change that?"

She laughed again. "The right man, as you say, is not likely to cross my path any time soon. I deal with families. When I'm home, I take advantage of living in New York and go to museums and galleries. I love living in New York. But I also love the Spanish riviera, the Carribean, the South Pacific, Mexico. I have the best life I could imagine."

He heard the enthusiasm in her voice. For a moment he envied her. She knew what she wanted and had gone after it. He had too, when Melissa had been alive. Now some days it seemed as if he was merely going through the motions. Staying on top of the firm and the competition used to afford a challenge he excelled in meeting. Now it was just what he did.

His flat was lonely in the evenings once the boys had gone to bed and Hannah retired to her quarters. He missed being part of couple, he realized suddenly. He had not thought about marrying again because of the pain of loss. But he missed having someone to talk to, make plans with, dream about a future with.

Would he ever meet a woman to chance marriage again? Would he ever risk his heart?

"It's getting cold here," she said, heading back toward the salon.

He turned watching her walk into the light. There was something intriguing about Stacey—she knew what she wanted and went all out to get it. What would the man be

like who could lure her from her chosen path to marry and build a family?

Luis had a feeling he wouldn't like him no matter who he was.

CHAPTER FIVE

THE next morning, Luis rose early. With the conversation of last night still echoing in his mind, he decided to spend the morning with his sons. He found them eating on the terrace with the other children. Stacey sat with Theresa at the adult table. It looked as if they'd become friends. The happiness about the new baby had shone from both his cousins since they'd arrived, and he expected Alli would love having a younger brother or sister.

"Good morning," he greeted the women. "Where is everyone?"

"Good morning, Luis," Theresa replied. "Jose is on some long-distance phone call, Abuela is having her breakfast in her room after that late night. Sophia's with her, I think. Don't know where Sebastian and Anna are."

"What's on the agenda for today?" he asked as he filled his plate from the lavish buffet near the house.

"Swimming this morning. We thought we'd go to town this afternoon. Depending on when Miguel and his family arrive and Isabella, we might stay home. That's the best part of vacation—no schedules," Theresa said.

Luis nodded, sitting down opposite Stacey. He looked at her. She looked fresh and appealing. Glancing over at the children's table, he tried to ignore the pull of attrac-

tion he felt when around her. The boys looked as if they were having the time of their lives. He was glad.

"Are you swimming with us today?" Stacey asked.

"I plan to spend the entire day with them," Luis said.

"They'll love that!" Stacey answered, a smile lighting up her face.

The morning passed swiftly. The boys were delighted when their father joined them and soon all three were playing in the sea. Theresa sat in the shade with Stacey, watching Jose and Allie play with the others. Anna's children were also part of the fun, but she and Sebastian had not come to the beach.

After lunch Luis asked Stacey to accompany him and the boys on a trip along the coast. "I want to revisit some old haunts and show them to the boys. There's a pretty village about ten miles up the coast that has some caves nearby. I thought they'd like to explore."

"Sounds great. If you're sure you want me along."

"Definitely. It's easier one on one, as I'm finding out." She grinned.

When they reached the village he had in mind, Stacey was charmed by it. The architecture was older than that of Alta Parisa, Moorish in design. There were blocky buildings that, when she could peek in through openings, gave way to large courtyards with water fountains and flowers galore.

They parked near the town center.

"Where're the caves?" Juan asked, having been told of their adventure.

"We walk from here. When we return, we'll stop at a sidewalk café for drinks," Luis said getting out of the car.

The walk through part of the town gave Stacey plenty

of time to enjoy the beauty of the place. They came to a well-worn path that led from the edge of town up a hill-side. About half a mile up, off the path about twenty-five yards, was a large cave with a wide opening. They scrambled over the brush and soon stood beneath the huge vault, turning to look at the view to the sea.

Stacey looked overhead. "What's holding this up?" she asked. To her it looked like a huge expanse of stone ready to drop and squash them all flat.

"The rock. It won't come down, if that's what you think," Luis said, studying the arch. "It's been here as long as the village and has never changed."

"Let's hope so. Still, I think I'll wait right over there while you all explore the cave," she said, pointing to a sunny spot several yards outside the cave.

"Chicken," Luis said.

She nodded emphatically. "And proud of it. At least if it squashes you I'll be around to tell everyone what happened."

"Happy thought."

Stacey was already moving out of the rocky cave to the solid earth. "I can watch from here," she called when she felt she was far enough away.

"Where's Stacey going?" Pablo asked.

"She wants to stay in the sunshine. Come on, I remember some ancient pictures on the walls in the back. Maybe from prehistoric man." Luis led the way, both boys excited about being in the cave.

It grew dimmer as they moved from the opening. A slight curve led to another chamber. Even in the dim light Luis found the pictorial drawings. Stick figures for the most part, he'd let his imagination run when he'd been a kid and explored the cave for the first time. Now it brought back memories he'd almost forgotten.

When the boys asked what they meant, he made up a story to account for them, delighting in their attention. He'd seen the cave on his own. What would he have given to have his father come with him, share the adventure?

When had he forgotten how much as a young boy he had wanted his parents during the summers, instead of being shunted off to stay with his grandparents?

"This is fun, Daddy," Pablo said.

"It is," Luis said. He felt a moment of panic when he thought how close he'd come to not responding to his grandmother's invitation. And his plans had once been to shunt them off on their nanny. He'd be as guilty as his father if he'd continued in that direction. He wouldn't want Juan and Pablo to grow up with some of the feelings he'd had as a teenager.

Really looking at his boys, he saw their individuality. True, they looked alike, but their personalities made it easy to differentiate between them. They looked like Melissa, but also a bit like himself. Mostly they looked like Juan and Pablo, the best parts of him and Melissa.

"Are there more caves?" Juan asked.

"Yes. If we continue up the path we were on, we'll come to another one, smaller, and no pictures. But cooler in the heat of the day. As I remember, there was cold air blowing from inside." He'd always wanted to find where that cold air was coming from, but by the time he had been old enough to truly go investigating, his interests had changed.

"Wow, I want to go there," Juan said.

They headed outside. Stacey sat on the ground, staring at the view. When she heard them behind her she jumped up and spun around.

"You're safe!"

Luis had to laugh. They'd been safe all along. He would never put his sons in danger.

"We're going to see a cave with cold air blowing," Juan said, running over to her. "And we saw pictures on the wall, stories for kids written on the walls because they didn't have books a long time ago."

She looked at Luis.

"There're some drawings inside that are thought to be from prehistoric times. You missed the story."

"But you were able to decipher it?"

"Of course." He winked at her. "We're continuing up the path. Come along. This time you might venture more than three feet inside."

"I was fine here," she said, falling into step with him as the boys ran ahead.

At one point the path was broken by stones. Luis went first, reaching back to help the boys across and then Stacey. Her hand gripped his as she gingerly walked over or around the rough stones. When she reached the other side, Luis was slow to release her hand. Startled, she looked into his eyes, and he felt a totally unexpected urge to lean over and kiss her.

For endless moments time seemed to stand still. Then Juan called impatiently and the spell was broken. He let her go and turned.

Stacey thankfully didn't say a word. Had they stayed like that much longer he believed he would have kissed her. Right in front of the boys, who would never keep silent about such an event.

"Where's the cave, Daddy?" Juan asked, looking all around.

"Farther along."

"I hope it does have a cool breeze," Stacey said. "I'm getting warmer by the minute."

So was Luis, walking beside her. But it wasn't due to the sun.

A few more minutes and the cave appeared. The boys ran ahead.

"Are they okay? There aren't any holes or anything they could fall into, are there?" she asked.

"No holes."

"It's cold!" Pablo yelled, jumping up and down.

When Luis and Stacey reached the cave, they found Pablo waiting at the entrance. The cool breeze coming from the cave was refreshing after the hot climb.

"I want to go inside, Daddy," Pablo said. Juan was already exploring the cave, yelling to hear his voice echo.

"I'll wait here," Stacey said, eyeing the cave with some wariness.

"It's safe, guaranteed," Luis said, responding to the tugging on his hand by Pablo.

"Go and enjoy," Stacey said.

She didn't mind waiting. She had a beautiful view to study, and could hear the murmur of their voices as Luis told the boys about his own childhood exploration of the cave.

She was glad he was spending the day with his sons. Children needed special time with their parents. Too often adults she worked for were caught up in business and social activities and didn't make time for their children. These boys would remember this vacation all their lives.

She wished she and Savannah had more happy memories of their childhood. But with an older grandmother constantly in pain with arthritis, their activities had been limited.

When they returned to town sometime later, Stacey relished sitting in the small café beneath a huge umbrella.

They had a view of the town square and she enjoyed watching people as they walked by, intent on their own errands, ignoring those taking a break at the sidewalk tables.

"This is fun, Daddy," Juan said, squirming around in his chair a lemonade in front of him. "Can we go swimming when we go back to Abuela's house?"

"We'll have to see. More family's arriving today. I don't know what Abuela Maria wants us to do."

"There're a lot of people in her house," Pablo said, sitting on the edge of his chair. "I don't like so many people."

"Once you know who everyone is, you'll feel more comfortable," Stacey said. "I don't have lots of relatives like you boys do. Just think how much you'll have to tell Hannah when you go home."

"What are rel'tives? Pablo asked.

"Family members. Like Abuela Maria—she's my grandmother, and your great-grandmother. You're related to her, as are your cousins."

"Like Alli?" he asked.

"Just like Alli." Luis looked at Stacey. "How much would they understand?"

"Probably not a lineage. Just say they're all cousins, or aunts and uncles. Things can be sorted out when they're older."

"And Stacey, is she a rel'tive?" Pablo asked.

"No, sweetie, just your nanny for this vacation," she said, hiding the hint of regret that she wasn't connected to these sweet boys for much longer than the three weeks of the assignment.

"Consider her a friend," Luis said, not meeting her eyes. The sooner they returned to the villa, the sooner he

could escape her tantalizing presence. Friendship was not what was lingering in his mind when it came to Stacey Williams.

The house seemed full of people when they returned. Stacey held back while Luis went to greet the newly arrived guests. The boys stood by her, watching with wide eyes. When Luis gestured them over, she gently patted their shoulders. "It'll be fine," she said. "Go and meet everybody."

Pablo reached for her hand. "There's too many."

She squeezed his hand gently and walked with him toward his father. "You'll get everyone straight in no time. You already know Sebastian and his family and Theresa and hers."

Luis introduced her to yet more cousins, Pedro and Miguel and their families. She was having trouble keeping everyone straight herself, so she knew the twins were. She tried to excuse herself once Pablo released her hand, but Luis urged her to stay. He merely told the others she was helping with the boys while they were in Spain.

She wondered why he didn't say she was the hired help. Now she caught a speculative glance here and there and knew people were trying to figure out where she fit in. She hoped they weren't thinking she and Luis were a couple. He'd hate that. She kept her distance—as much as her employer would allow.

At a break in the conversation, Stacey said she was taking the boys for a quick swim. They'd become restless and she knew the adult conversation was over their heads. Their other younger cousins were nowhere to be seen.

Once on the beach, the boys ran to the sea. Pedro and

Paloma and Alli were already in the water. The maid who had first greeted them watched the children.

After dinner, she took the boys upstairs to bath and get ready for bed. They went right to bed without a fuss, tired from all the activities.

"Today was fun," Juan said as he settled beneath the sheet.

"I was afraid in the cave, but Daddy showed me the drawings. And he said it was not a scary place, but nice to get out of the sun," Pablo said.

"That's right. And lots of history," Stacey said, settling in next to Pablo, ready to read them their nightly book.

"What's history?" Juan asked.

"The story of what happened before," she replied.

"So living in New York is history."

"What happened before you came here is history. The future will be when you go back home."

"What else is history?"

"Everything that's already happened. Even our trip to the cave is history. Now, settle down and let's read this book."

When the boys had fallen asleep she debated going downstairs or to her room. It was still too early to go to bed, but she felt awkward joining the family as if she were a guest instead of the boys' nanny. Slipping quietly down the stairs, she went out to the garden. There were low lights illuminating the paths and benches placed periodically where one could sit and enjoy the flowers.

She found a secluded nook and sat on the stone bench, soaking up the sweet fragrances of the flowers, the coolness of the night air. She wondered where her sister was tonight. She would have returned from her Alaska cruise

by now; she probably had gone out on another assignment already. Requests were coming in faster and faster now. They might have to consider hiring another nanny or two if their business continued to grow.

Stacey hoped Savannah got an assignment as relaxing as this one was. She loved the sea. Maybe she'd walk along the shore.

Jumping up to do that, she was startled when Luis spoke behind her.

"I wondered if you'd gone to bed," he said.

She turned. "No. Just enjoying the garden. I thought I'd take a walk along the shore. There's enough light from the moon and stars so I won't walk into anything. I could almost read by the bright light from the moon tonight."

"I'll join you," Luis said. He'd enjoyed seeing his cousins and their families again. It had been a number of years since they'd all be together, so there was plenty of catching up to do. Yet at the first opportunity he'd slipped out, searching for Stacey.

He frowned as they walked through the garden to the beach. He had gone looking for her—to make sure she was all right. She had not returned after putting his children to bed. His grandmother had told him at one point to make sure Stacey knew she was to be included in the adult activities.

When he'd told her Stacey was hired to watch his sons, she'd countered that they needed no watching when asleep.

It wouldn't hurt to humor her. It wasn't as if it was a hardship. Stacey was easily the most comfortable person to be around. She made no demands and had no false expectations. She liked who she was and what she was doing.

As did he.

The beach was empty, only the soft sound of the small waves rushing onto shore could be heard. The lights from the villa grew dimmer as they walked. The next villa was dark, giving a wide expanse of beach lit only by the moon and stars.

"I'm surprised you don't come here every year," Stacey said as they walked. "Your grandmother is enjoying your visit."

"When they were younger, I felt they were too young for the long flights. Then the last couple of years I've been busier than ever at work." Luis frowned again as he thought of how much time he spent at the office. His children were growing fast and if he didn't cut back his hours, he'd miss their childhood altogether. "Perhaps, knowing how well they're doing this summer, we can return each year. And include you each summer? Hannah's not likely to change her mind about flying."

"We fill up fast, so book early."

"Maybe I'll reserve your services as soon as we return to New York."

"Great, it's always good to have jobs lined up. Makes for security," she said.

"Don't you get tired of living out of suitcase all year long? Never home for holidays or special anniversaries?" he countered.

"Um. Sometimes it gets old—especially at the end of the summer when I'm finally finished with back-to-back assignments."

He wondered at the hesitation.

"So?" he pressed.

"So maybe, lately, I might wish to change things a bit."

Before he could question her more, he heard a call behind them.

"Luis, wait!"

They turned to see Sebastian and Anna walking toward them.

"I see we all had the same idea. Fun though family is, a bit of quiet before bed is welcomed," Sebastian said when they reached Luis and Stacey.

"I love being at the beach," Anna said. "The flat we have in Madrid has a garden, but nothing like this. It's surrounded by other buildings and only gets sun when it's overhead. I love the space here at the villa and the endless beach."

Stacey asked more about their flat and Anna described it in detail as they walked along. Soon the men outpaced the women.

"I hope it was all right we joined you," Anna asked when Luis and Sebastian had gone ahead.

"Of course. Why wouldn't it be?" Stacey asked.

"I didn't want to intrude. But Sebastian wanted to talk to Luis. They were very close as boys."

"There's nothing to intrude into," Stacey said. "You know I'm the boys' nanny, nothing more."

"If you say so. I'm glad he's doing so well. He's been lonely since his wife died. This is his first visit here in years. He needs to fall in love again and get married."

"You need to talk to him about that," Stacey said. She could imagine Luis's reaction if she brought that up.

"Oh, no, not me. Maybe Sebastian or Jose. Or even Isabella when she gets here. I think that's why Abuela pairs him with you sometimes. I think she wants him to see the advantages of being part of a couple again and maybe begin dating when he returns home."

Stacey nodded, thankful no one seemed to see how much she wished part of that couple could be her.

"Maybe he'll realize that all on his own. He strikes me as a very smart man," she said.

"How do you like the boys."

"I think they're adorable." Stacey told Anna about some of the antics they'd been up to since she'd met them. Anna shared some stories of her children and soon they were both laughing.

Luis could hear the women behind them. He knew they didn't realize how voices carried at night. It was easy for Anna to say he should date, get married again. She hadn't had a searing loss of a spouse. She hadn't had the daunting task of raising two young infants, trying to build a business, trying to balance everything in life. Much as he hated to admit it, he was afraid to fall in love, afraid to be at the mercy of whatever tragedy might unfold. The initial agony of Melissa's passing had eased. But he could still feel the knife like pain that had pierced his heart.

Melissa's death had been unexpected and unforeseen. But so would a traffic fatality or a plane crash. There were so many things to go wrong, how had mankind ever made it this far?

"Don't listen to them," Sebastian said.

"What?"

"I heard, too. Anna's not the quietest of women. That's what's made you go silent, right?" Sebastian said in a low voice.

"It was impossibly hard to lose Melissa."

"You'll never find a first love again," Sebastian said. "You've made a good life for yourself and your twins. You have them to look to for family. One day grandchildren. Many never get that."

"I know, and I am grateful. But sometimes I wonder..." Luis fell silent. He wasn't going to share his

doubts with his cousin on how he was doing as a father. There was nothing Sebastian could do about the doubts, so no need to tell him.

"I wonder what the future holds as well. We won't know until we get there."

Luis didn't correct his assumptions.

They turned around and Luis felt a pang of envy when Anna smiled at her husband and came to join him, linking her hand in his. "It's time to go back. It's getting cooler and we'll be up early with the children."

"We're going to Guadelest tomorrow. Want to join us?" Sebastian said.

Luis looked at Stacey, then away. He did not need to consult her. "Yes. I know the boys'll love it. Remember the games we played there?"

"Sure do. I think you were last king, right?"

Luis nodded. "Now a new generation gets to play."

"Ah, it's a bit more crowded than when we played there. Still, we'll see," Sebastian said.

Sebastian and Anna quickened their pace, taking the lead. Stacey fell in beside Luis. "What did that mean, you were last king?"

"Guadelest is an old Moorish fortress, build to defend the valley. We used to play there when we were kids, to see who won and got to be king. Last time we played as young teenagers, I won. Then next couple of summers Sebastian didn't visit and by the time he came again, our interests had changed dramatically—then we wanted to dance with girls and see who could have the most fun at fiesta."

"Sounds like typical boys. Just think, your own boys will be that age one day, and will probably cause heartbreak for all the girls—especially when they find out they live in America and are only visiting."

"I don't even want to think that far ahead. They're only six. I need for them to stay little boys as long as they can."

"Kids have a way of growing up."

That's what Luis was afraid of.

Luis watched as Stacey went up stairs a short time later. He considered joining the rest of the family still talking in the salon, but decided to head for bed himself. He wasn't used to having so much free time. He preferred the driving force of work and the routine he and the boys had in New York.

Yet the free time gave him a chance to think about things normally relegated to a back burner. He needed to spend more time with Juan and Pablo. He smiled, thinking about their afternoon together. They'd loved the caves. As he had as a child. Their childish observations at the café had been funny.

There was something to be said for his grandmother's family reunion idea. Still—in the morning, he needed to make a quick run to the internet café and touch base with the office before they went to Guadelest.

The trip to the old Moorish fortress was fun for the boys and Stacey. Luis and Sebastian regaled everyone about their adventures when they'd been kids. What areas they had explored, what games they'd played. Anna and Sebastian's kids were as fascinated as Luis's boys were to learn their father had played kings in the old town when younger. Only a few days in Spain and already Juan and Pablo had picked up enough Spanish to get along with their newly met cousins. Once they reached the fortress, they ran and pretended to be defending the fort.

Luis watched, memories crowding in. He'd missed his family the last few years. But he couldn't help a pang

of envy, watching Sebastian and Anna. Their closeness was something else he missed and hadn't realized how much until now.

They returned to the villa in time for lunch, and to greet the last of the guests to arrive, including Luis's parents and sister Isabella. He was glad his father had made the effort to visit at his mother's request. So many summers in the past she'd asked him to stay when he had brought Luis and Isabella. He'd always have a reason to refuse.

The twins hardly knew their grandparents and, after greeting them, took off with Sebastian's children. Stacey met them, then went to supervise the children at the beach.

"What happened to the other nanny?" Carlos Aldivista asked his son.

"Hannah has a fear of flying I never knew about. She refused to come. Stacey's temporary, just for the vacation," Luis explained.

"She's young," his mother commented.

"Older than she looks and highly qualified," Luis said. Hadn't he had the same thoughts?

"If you'd remarry, you wouldn't need a nanny."

He nodded. He'd heard that idea more the last couple of days than the entire time since his wife's death.

"You'll enjoy getting to know Stacey," his grandmother said, joining the threesome. "She speaks Spanish very well, though with a slight accent. And she's traveled the world almost as much as you have."

"How do you know that?" Carlos asked.

"Because I asked her and she told me. She and I talk sometimes when the children are in bed."

"Isn't she the nanny?" Marguerita asked.

"That's her job, it doesn't exclude her from other ac-

tivities when the boys don't need her," Maria said. She narrowed her gaze at her son and daughter-in-law. "It wouldn't hurt you two to spend more times with your grandsons, you know."

"*Sí*," Carlos said, glancing at his wife with resignation.

Luis knew his parents had never been loving and nurturing, like some. But they were honest, hard-working and had instilled strong work ethics in their children. Still—how often had he longed for more attention from his father or a kinder word from his mother?

With a shock he realized even more clearly he was in danger of becoming like his father. When as a child he'd protested about being left with his grandmother when school was out, wasn't he virtually putting his own sons in second place behind work on a daily basis?

"If you'll excuse me, I think I'll join the twins on the beach."

As he walked away, Luis heard his mother ask if it was the boys or the pretty nanny that enticed him to the beach.

He wished he could have heard his grandmother's response. Or maybe he should have turned and answered his mother himself. Since the first day when they'd learned to swim, he'd realized how much of their lives he'd missed. Granted, Hannah shared the milestones with him—when they'd first walked, first got a tooth.

But she didn't talk about their first words, what scared them in the night, or what they loved to do above all else. They were six, and he'd already missed a third of the time they'd live with him. Not only had he enjoyed teaching them to swim, he'd enjoyed them every day since.

Maybe he should give Stacey the afternoon off to show his mother it was his sons he wanted to spend time

with. He was going to have to make that a priority. He was good at setting priorities and following through.

But he wouldn't give Stacey the time off—she made everything so much more fun, for both him and the boys. Could he bring that kind of joy to the afternoon on his own? She had a special knack of seeing everything in a new and positive way. She made the most mundane event sparkle. Luis wasn't immune to wanting some of that sparkle for himself.

When Luis arrived at the beach, all the children were in the water, along with Stacey, Anna and Theresa, the only adults with them. Watching Juan and Pablo yelling and laughing, he felt a pang of regret. Then shook it off. If he had his way, he'd make sure they only had good times to remember in the future. Stacey was good for them. Whatever magic she had was working. He had not had a complaint from either of the boys, or anyone else in the family. Their behavior was exemplary. Stacey made it seem easy.

He dropped his towel and went to join them.

"We're playing diving for treasure, Daddy," Juan called when he spotted his father. "I won a piece of eight!"

"Wow, from a Spanish galleon?" Luis asked, wondering if it really was gold.

"Huh?" Juan obviously hadn't a clue what a Spanish galleon was.

Stacey and Anna laughed.

"We found these old fake coins at the market the other day and Stacey suggested we throw them in the water for the kids to retrieve," Theresa explained. She held up the golden-colored coin and then flipped it over her shoulder. Immediately all the children dived in behind

her, searching for the coin. Juan and Pablo were right in the thick of things.

"To think a few days ago they had never gone swimming, now they dive for treasure," he murmured. Once again the clutch of emotion hit. He'd almost missed it. He vowed then and there to do better. To be a better father to his sons.

"They're having a grand time, warriors by morning, divers this afternoon," Stacey said, watching them. "And the one with the most coins gets to choose the next game."

He looked at her. She was having as much fun as the children, laughing with them, shouting hooray when someone stood up, proudly holding the coin. He could watch her all afternoon. An involuntary smile came. She had more enthusiasm than anyone else he knew. No wonder she was so liked by her charges, she brought magic to their lives.

And in the evenings after the boys had gone to bed and she joined the adults, she fit in perfectly. He already knew his grandmother enjoyed talking with her. It surprised him a bit to hear her praise Stacey to his parents. He hadn't noticed a special attachment growing.

When the children had retrieved all the coins, Pedro had the most and proposed a race. Luis agreed to swim out, Stacey would give the "go" signal and the first to reach Luis would win. Though it was unlikely the younger children would beat Pedro or Paloma, still, everyone was excited and soon the water was splashing and churning as they all raced toward Luis.

The afternoon passed swiftly and almost before they knew it, it was time to go in to get ready for dinner.

Luis walked back to the villa beside Stacey. "I predict two tired little boys tonight."

She nodded, watching them trudge toward the villa. "You're right. I expect they'll have a hard time keeping awake through dinner. They've had a full day. Fun, though."

"And did you have fun?" he asked.

"Of course. I enjoyed seeing the old fortress and watching the boys play with their cousins. This afternoon furthered that bond. If you return every year, they'll build ties so strong they'll never be severed." She looked wistfully at the children.

"And you have no cousins, right?"

"Only my sister. We're very close, but it's quiet when we spend holidays together."

"All the more reason to have a houseful of kids. And if your husband comes from a large family, you'll have big celebrations like this one." Luis wondered what she'd look for in a husband. Again the idea struck that he wouldn't like any man who Stacey might fall in love with.

"Well, I don't know if I could handle as many guests at one time as are here. Your grandmother has everything running perfectly. I'm like the boys, afraid there are too many people to keep them all straight. Fortunately, I don't need to. I can always slip out to the garden and enjoy the evening quiet while the rest of you catch up on family news."

He'd like to slip out with Stacey. He should visit with his parents, find out what his sister had been up to these last few months since he'd seen her. But he wanted to be with Stacey.

"Tell you what, after the boys are in bed, meet me in the garden and we'll take off for the village. There used to be a bar there with a band that's well worth listening to."

Stacey looked at him in surprise. "Can you do that?"

"What, go to a bar? I'm old enough."

She shook her head, smiling. "I meant get away. Your parents just arrived, don't you want to spend time with them?"

"You'll find that there isn't a lot to be said between my parents and me. My father doesn't understand me and I don't understand him. We're fine with that."

"Hmm."

"Hey, every family isn't perfect like you see on TV."

"I know, but I thought if only my parents had lived, I'd have the perfect family. You're shattering that dream."

"And maybe you would have. Or maybe not."

"True." She glanced at him, taking a risk. "Okay, I'll meet you in the garden after I put the twins to bed."

"It's a date."

CHAPTER SIX

IT WAS not a date, Stacey told herself as she tucked the boys in early and read them a short story. It was just Luis's way of showing her a bit more of Alta Parisa.

But her giddy reaction belied her true feelings. She was going out with Luis Aldivista! Just the two of them.

Once the boys fell asleep, Stacey raced to her room to check her appearance one more time. The sun dress was the same blue as her eyes. Old as it was, it was her favorite. She'd been told more than once how pretty she looked in it. She hoped Luis thought so as well. Running a brush through her hair, she noticed how much lighter it was from her days in the sun. Thanks to the sun screen she slathered on, her skin was only lightly tanned, but enhanced her eyes even more. Smiling, she saw the excitement reflected there.

She took a deep breath then twirled around the room before heading downstairs. The murmur from the salon told her where everyone was—even Luis? Had he made his escape yet?

She went out the front door and around to the side, not wanting anyone to stop her if seen.

Twilight had fallen. It was still light enough to see, yet full darkness wouldn't be far away. She went to the

bench she liked. Luis sat there, watching the path, and spotted her when she rounded the large shrub.

"I didn't know if you'd be here," she said a little breathlessly. He looked amazing. The sun had darkened his skin, lightened his hair. His fair coloring still surprised her.

"I didn't want to get into a long-winded discussion of the dangers of the internet, which my father started. Easier to just fade away." He stood. "Ready?"

She nodded.

He reached out and took her hand. The gesture surprised her. As did the tingling that coursed through her with his touch. Linking their fingers together, he led the way around the back of the house and to the garage. In less than five minutes they were driving into the village. Stacey felt like a kid playing hooky—excited and daring. Parking near the town square, Luis took her hand again when she alighted from the car. They walked through the quiet streets to the bar. Part sidewalk café, the outer doors were huge glass ones that opened completely to the inside. The *Estella de España* was already crowded with people of all ages. Young children ran around. Older couples sat and watched indulgently. Teenagers flirted and parents scolded, then laughed.

"We're a bit early. They don't start playing until nine," he said, signaling the waiter. When they were seated at a small table on the sidewalk, Stacey looked around with delight. "This is amazing. I didn't realize what a family place this was. We could have brought the twins."

"Not tonight, they would have fallen asleep in no time. These kids have siestas."

"As your grandmother and Sophia do every day. Maybe we should adopt that custom," she replied.

"It drove me crazy when I was here as a kid. But they

keep later hours than we do in the States, so the nap's needed. Better not to get used to it."

"Right, just as soon as I'd get used to a siesta every day, I'll be back on a new assignment and probably not to Spain."

He nodded. Their orders were taken. Then the musicians came onto the small stage set near the wide opening of the building.

"They run this place rain or shine, but don't want to risk getting the instruments wet," Luis said, nodding to their position. It was perfect for all those present. There were two guitars, a keyboard, a saxophone and a set of drums. When the men picked up their instruments, the crowd cheered. Soon the music began. It was fast and lively and totally unfamiliar to Stacey. Which did nothing to dim her enjoyment.

"This is great," she said.

Their beverages were served and she took a sip. It was delightful to be free of her duties for a little while. With only the hint of guilt. Should she be with her employer? She glanced around and noted some of the looks other women were giving Luis. Smugly pleased he'd chosen to spend his evening with her, she vowed he wouldn't regret it. And she wasn't going to either!

Some of the other customers got up to dance. The teenagers seemed to be having a great time. Little children mimicked them, darting away when they got a frowning look, laughing the entire time. Soon a few adults joined the small dance floor.

The next two songs were familiar, then a slow song played.

"Care to dance?" Luis asked, watching the older couples take to the floor.

"Sure." Stacey loved to dance. And that was some-

thing that didn't happen often. When was the last time she'd been on a date? Last Halloween? Ages ago.

When he took her into his arms, he rested his cheek against her forehead. The slow music was haunting. The touch of his fingers on her back above the edge of the sun dress warmed her like a fire. Moving with him, she closed her eyes and for a short time let herself imagine they were a couple. That this was one of many nights together, dancing, being with each other. She felt cherished when he blocked their bumping into another couple. The floor was small and crowded but with her eyes closed she could imagine the two of them were alone in the world.

The song went on and on and as if as reluctant to end as she was reluctant to have it end. When it did, there was a moment of silence, then applause. The next song was fast again. Luis didn't leave the floor.

Dancing the night away would rank up there as one of her best memories of any assignment.

It was after one when Stacey caught sight of the time.

"Goodness, those boys get up early. I need to get some sleep tonight."

"One more dance, then we'll head home."

She smiled—pleased he seemed as loath to leave as she did. But after a full day of sightseeing and playing in the sea, she was starting to feel tired. "Okay, one more."

The lively number had them breathing hard when finished. She'd wished for another slow song, but they were few and far between.

The ride back to the villa was made in silence. Stacey felt as if she was floating on a cloud. If she weren't so tired, she could have wished the night to last until dawn.

"I had a marvelous time," she said when the villa

came into view. Only one light remained on downstairs. Someone must have noticed they'd gone out.

She grinned. "I feel like a teenager sneaking in late."

"At least they left a light on so we don't stumble in the dark," he said, stopping the car near the front door. "I'll park this around the back tomorrow. Let's hope they left the door unlocked."

Quietly entering the house through the unlocked door, they headed for the stairs. Luis switched off the light in the salon and followed Stacey up the wide stairs. He walked her to her door, passing his along the way.

"Thanks for coming. I enjoyed the evening," he said.

"Me, too. Thanks for inviting me along," she said, reaching out for the doorknob. Luis stopped her. Cupping her chin with one hand, he bent down and kissed her.

A thousand warning bells clanged in her mind, but she ignored them all. She wanted this. And it was heaven. His lips pressed against hers. She breathed in his scent, her heart racing. Just before she reached out to draw him closer, he pulled back, his eyes gazing into hers.

"You're very special, Stacey. Thanks for taking such good care of my twins."

The words splashed through like icy water. She felt her smile falter. "You're most welcome. Goodnight." She slipped into her room, shut the door and leaned against it, wanting to bang her head against the wood.

"Idiot, what did you expect?" she asked herself in frustration. "That the man would fall for a nanny? He was making sure the nanny continued to watch is kids after a night off for good behavior."

She pushed away and went to get ready for bed, constantly telling herself not to read *anything* into a goodnight kiss. He hadn't even hugged her, just cupped her face. It meant nothing, just a nice end to the evening.

But once beneath the covers, it was all Stacey could do not to relive the special sensations that had flooded through her with his kiss. She had felt love surging up and spilling over.

Shocked, she shook her head. Not love. Lust maybe. Face it, he was one sexy man. But not for her.

That was the mantra she recited until she finally fell asleep only a short time before dawn.

Stacey would have given anything to avoid Luis the next morning. She hoped he had no hint how that kiss had rocked her world. He was a man, what did he care about emotions and feelings and crushes? It was probably just a reflex at the end of a night out. She'd kissed at the end of other dates.

But none with the effect of this one.

Fortunately, Luis was not at the breakfast table when Stacey had the boys dressed and downstairs. She served herself and went to sit at the children's table. Time to establish firm boundaries lest Luis think she was angling for more than a nanny position.

Only he didn't show up so missed her silent declaration. Abuela Maria joined them at the children's table, much to Stacey's surprise.

"I love children," the older woman said in answer to Stacey's look. "With segregated tables, I don't get to hear their conversations as much as I like."

Soon all the children had arrived and were enthralled to have their great-grandmother sitting with them. Stacey enjoyed the stories she told, thinking a couple of times of her own grandmother and the family stories she'd told. She missed her more and more as time went by.

Keeping an eye out for Luis, however, she wasn't as subtle as she hoped.

"Luis went to the internet café, he won't be home for a while," Abuela Maria said.

"Oh." Stacey smiled wryly. So much for trying to look unconcerned.

"Despite his faithful attendance at that café, he's spending time with the children. I think he's relaxing more and more." She studied Stacey for a moment. "And I think it's due to you."

"No. He loves the boys. I think he's happy for the break, even though he's having trouble letting go completely," Stacey said, hoping the heat in her cheeks didn't flush them.

"All work is not good. Now he needs to re-examine his life and make some changes for the better."

Stacey refused to even speculate on what she meant.

Luis stared at the computer screen. He'd been gazing at it for several minutes, not registering a single word. Again and again he relived the goodnight kiss he'd given Stacey. He hadn't been a monk since Melissa's death but he'd only dated for short periods of time and made sure each woman knew from the beginning he was not interested in a long-term relationship. Most had been fine with that as they'd wanted to make their mark in Manhattan before settling down.

If a woman wanted more, he quickly ended the relationship.

But Stacey was different. She'd already woven herself into his life. His grandmother liked her. The boys adored her. For the first time he could remember, they behaved without throwing tantrums or causing disturbances that had him loathing to take them anywhere. Even Hannah didn't have the rapport with them that Stacey had.

Her lips had been soft and sweet. The contact had electrified him. He wanted more.

Yet how could he begin dating his boys' nanny? There'd be so many complications.

He had a certain personal code and one of his tenets had been not to date a coworker or employee. On the other hand, Stacey wasn't a long-time employee—there were only a couple of weeks left of the vacation and then she'd no longer work for him.

He took a sip of coffee. It had grown cold. Glancing at his watch, he was surprised to see how much time had passed. With so little accomplished.

Focusing on the email, he quickly sent a reply. Signaling the waiter for another coffee, he looked out the wide window facing the square. Some people hurried by, obviously caught up in their daily tasks. Others sauntered, gazing into windows, no doubt on vacation. Enjoying themselves without a worry in the world.

What was he going to do about Stacey and the growing desire he had for her?

The prudent thing would be to keep his distance. She was there for Juan and Pablo, not for him.

But the hunger in him had him devising ways to spend time with her. It didn't matter if the boys were with them. She brought sunshine to the day, whatever they were doing. He liked listening to her slightly accented Spanish. Her laughter was infectious. She brought enthusiasm to everything.

And she danced divinely.

He took the coffee when it came and left the computer to the next customer, choosing a table that overlooked the street. Thinking about her wasn't getting him anywhere. He wanted to see her again.

* * *

Half an hour later Luis walked out onto the beach where the entire household seemed gathered. Children played in the water, numerous umbrellas offered shade to those not in the sea. Lounge chairs took up all the shady space, with one or two vacant in the sun.

He spotted Stacey immediately. She was in the water with the children and once again they seemed to be diving for treasure. He dropped his towel on one of the vacant chairs as he greeted those on the beach then headed for the sea, the sand hot beneath his feet. He might wish to spend time alone with Stacey, but for now, any time together would be worthwhile.

He dived into the water once he was out far enough and swam to where they played. Stacey greeted him with the same smile she normally did—or was there a hint of strain in it?

"Busy working?" she asked, dodging Juan's attempt to grab a coin while she was distracted.

"Catching up. Now it's time for play."

"You can help toss treasure," she said, opening her left hand and showing him the bunch of coins. When he took some, his fingers brushed against her palm. He heard the soft intake of her breath and looked into her eyes. She quickly looked away. Once he had the coins she spun around and called another challenge to the children.

So maybe he wasn't the only one affected by their kiss. He wanted another just to see what happened.

The day set the pattern for the rest of the week. With everyone having arrived for the celebration, there was plenty of time to visit with parents, cousins, children. Luis spent more time with his own parents than he had in recent years, catching up with their travels and trying to explain what his company did. With his sister's

arrival their family was complete. They didn't have the closeness he observed with his cousins, but there was a lot to be said for getting together once in a blue moon.

Yet something was missing. Sometimes at mealtimes when others were paired up with their spouses, he felt the loss even more. The nights Stacey sat beside him allowed him the luxury of pretending he was part of a couple. She didn't sit with the adults every night, however. In fact, he felt she was avoiding him as much as possible without causing comment.

To Luis's annoyance, she spent more time with the children than before. When he asked her to go to the bar again after dinner one night, she came up with an excuse that rang with insincerity.

He backed off for a few days, but after church on Sunday, which they all attended and helped to fill the small building in the village, he cornered Stacey, who was holding Pablo's hand.

"I want you and the boys to come with me for lunch. Family is fine, but you can have too much of a good thing."

She nodded.

Thankfully the awkwardness of earlier in the week had passed. He'd tread more cautiously now but he still would have another kiss. Or two.

"And where do you plan to eat?" she asked.

"At the café in Segundo."

"You're the boss. We're not going into caves again, are we?"

"Not dressed like this. We'll sit at the marina and watch the boats. The fishermen won't have sailed today, but lots of Sunday sailors will be out."

Luis let his grandmother know their plans and was gratified when the four of them set off a short time later,

Stacey sitting in the front beside him as he drove the rented car.

"I can't believe this weather," she commented, gazing out the window for the glimpses of the sea as they sped along the shore road. "It hasn't rained a single day we've been here."

"That probably won't last, but if it does rain I hope it won't during the fiesta. Have you ever been to a fiesta before? Will you come with me?"

"Since this is my first trip to Spain, what do you think?" She glanced at him. "Are you inviting me or me and the boys?"

"During the day, all of us, and into the evening, until the fireworks are over. Then you and me."

She studied him for a long moment. Luis flicked a glance at her and then back to the road. Suddenly he realized he'd be more than disappointed if she refused. He almost held his breath, awaiting her decision.

"I'd love to," she said at long last.

"What's a fiesta?" Pablo asked.

"Like a village party," Luis replied. "You'll love it. There's lots of booths with things for sale, some for display. Cotton candy."

"I love cotton candy," Juan said. "We get it every time Hannah takes us to the zoo."

Luis nodded.

Stacey looked at him and he shrugged. He instinctively knew what that look meant—he should be the one taking his sons to the zoo. Yet the last time he and the boys had gone out together without Hannah, it had been a disaster. Before they left Spain, he'd ask Stacey for her secret.

The café they'd visited before was crowded, but after only a short wait a table near the water opened up. They

ordered a light lunch. While they waited the boys kept asking questions about the boats they could see, if they were going climbing, if they would return home in time to swim.

Stacey looked at Luis. He was struck by the blue of her eyes, almost the color of the sea behind her. Her hair was getting lighter by the day. And that infectious smile had him ready to smile in anticipation of whatever she had to say.

"You're creating major expectations, you know that, right?"

"By that you mean?"

"By the time they return home to New York, they'll feel it odd not to swim every day. Does your apartment building have a pool?"

Luis shook his head. "We can try for the beach on weekends." For the first time, Luis realized he was looking forward to planning activities with Juan and Pablo. And he owed it all to Stacey. If she hadn't shown him how much being with the boys could mean, he'd probably have continued putting them behind work until they were grown and gone.

"That won't be the same. Don't forget half of New York heads for the beach on summer weekends. Here they have an endless sandy beach with hardly anyone on them. And the sea is so gentle and buoyant, not like the surf at Rockaway or Coney Island."

"They'll be seasoned swimmers by then. Do you go to the beach often?"

"Summer's our busiest time. I'm rarely in New York long enough to do laundry, much less take a day at the beach," Stacey said. "But if I could, I'd have my house there, remember?"

For the first time ever, Luis considered moving from

New York. The boys were blossoming here. Family rallied around. He wondered if he could move his company to Spain and operate out of Alta Parisa, taking the necessary trips to the States when business required.

Lunch arrived and for the next few minutes Stacey was busy helping the boys get started on their meal.

"Do you have your next assignment?" He wondered if he could conjure up another trip and engage her services.

"Not that I know of. But Stephanie could be booking my time right now. Usually I don't find out until I'm back. No distractions from the current job that way. Like with this job. I only found out the morning of our interview."

"What if we extend our trip?" he asked.

"Depends. If there's someone else to take on the next assignment, I could stay. But if not, our contract was for three weeks and I'd have to ask you to honor that."

He nodded. He'd have his secretary check in the morning. But time could be running out.

He'd thought about their night dancing—and that kiss—each evening as he retired to his lonely bed. She was in the room next door, but she might as well be a million miles away. If there was going to be a change in their relationship, he'd have to instigate it. If that's what he wanted. Normally he tried to foresee the ramifications of decisions to be made. But he couldn't see beyond today with Stacey. Did he want to risk taking their relationship to the next level?

"Let's go out to dinner together tonight. You and me, no boys, no other relatives, just the two of us," he said.

She met his gaze, her eyes thoughtful, conflicted.

"Why?"

"I like spending time with you." That would win the

understatement of the year award. He yearned to spend time with her. To lose himself in her eyes. To feel the excitement being near her brought. To consider when and how they'd share their next kiss.

Her sunny smile broke out. "I like being with you," she said. "But I feel odd, relinquishing my responsibilities to take personal time."

"You haven't had a day off since you started."

"Ah, but Vacation Nannies don't need a day off. Our days off come between assignments. That way we can give full service to those we work for."

"An evening off isn't such a big thing. Theresa or Anna would watch the boys if we asked. Abuela Maria has maids who could babysit."

"Okay, then. It sounds like fun."

He nodded, wondering if he'd misread her reaction last week. Maybe he should have pushed earlier for more evenings spent together.

After lunch the four of them strolled through the town. Stacey bought a scarf for her sister and a small snow globe of the village for Stephanie, Vacation Nannies' office manager.

The boys picked out a large photograph of the harbor to take home to Hannah.

On the drive back to the villa the boys fell asleep.

"I'll ask Theresa to keep an eye on them this evening, and let my grandmother know we won't be at dinner. I know a great seafood place up the coast. At least it was great the last time I was there. I'll see if anyone knows if it's still open," Luis said. He was looking forward to the evening. In fact, he could hardly wait. For the first time in years he felt carefree and full of anticipation.

* * *

Stacey spent a little extra time getting ready for the evening. She wore the same black dress she'd worn before, not having brought a wide selection. Who would have thought she'd be asked out twice? This was definitely a date. There were no two ways to look at it. Anticipation rose as she considered whether maybe they'd dance. Maybe he'd kiss her goodnight again. Heart tripping, she stared at herself in the mirror. And if he did, this time she wouldn't be caught by surprise and would kiss him back!

The blood hummed through her veins as she descended the stairs a bit later. She walked into the salon and met the gaze of Marguerita Aldivista. Glancing around, Stacey almost sighed when she saw it was just the two of them. She had not spent much time with Luis's mother.

She beckoned her over to sit beside her on one of the love seats. The rich gold brocade was as comfortable to sit on as it was pleasing to look at. But Stacey didn't feel comfortable at all.

"Maria tells me you and Luis are going out to dinner tonight," Marguerita said, raising an eyebrow in silent question.

"To a seafood place he knows," Stacey confirmed. Did his mother disapprove?

"*Mar Y Llevant* is about ten miles from here. Excellent choice. The restaurant's partially over the sea, anchored to land. The food's always perfectly prepared. You'll enjoy it."

Stacey longed to ask her if she disapproved of Luis dating his sons' nanny, but didn't know how to frame the question.

"He's been lonely, I think," Marguerita said pensively, looking beyond Stacey to the view of the sea.

"Luis?"

"He works too hard. Takes after his father in that regard. And with his job, there isn't the traveling that gives a break."

"Traveling gives a break?" It was the first Stacey heard of it.

"Carlos has to talk to me when we're on the plane," Marguerita said with a mischievous smile, her gaze returning to Stacey.

Stacey laughed. "As Luis talks to us in the car. Why do men get so caught up in work?"

"I've never figured that out. Being here has been very good for my son, I think. He was a bit neglected as a child—at least from my point of view. But when given the choice, I chose to go with his father. Luis and Isabella were well cared for here. As I remember, after the first day or two of each vacation they both had a wonderful time."

Stacey gained a little insight into Luis's mother. Maybe she'd been too quick to judge his parents.

"He speaks fondly of his summers here," she agreed.

"Ready?" Luis asked from the doorway.

"Yes." Stacey rose and impulsively gave Marguerita a hug. "I'll let you know how the food is."

The drive was quiet until they reached the shore highway.

"What were you and my mother talking about?" Luis asked.

"I think she missed a lot of your childhood and regrets it," Stacey said.

"She said that?"

"Sort of—I think that's what she feels now. You and your sister have a great extended family. You're lucky to know all your cousins and aunts and uncles. If you'd

stayed at home in the States as you were growing up, you'd have missed knowing them and would never be as close as you are now."

"Still doesn't mean I wouldn't have liked to have my parents around more."

"And it sounds as if your mother might have that same wish, now. Still, you can make anything work if you want it enough," she said.

"Even a long-distance relationship with someone who travels all the time?"

CHAPTER SEVEN

STACEY looked at him in surprise. "Such as your father does?" she asked.

"No, I meant you. I'd like to see you after we return home," he said.

"Why?"

"Why what?"

"Why would you want to see me? Not for the boys, they'll have Hannah."

He nodded, but didn't respond right away. Finally he said, "I've dated infrequently since Melissa died. Usually more when I needed an escort to some kind of professional event than for fun. I think I forgot how to just have fun." He glanced at her. "You bring fun to all you do. I like that."

She smiled but her heart dropped. He just wanted a friend, someone to have fun with. It most definitely didn't sound like a long-range plan that might one day lead to marriage. Maybe it was because she was getting closer to thirty, but now Stacey wanted more from life than she'd enjoyed these past five years.

"We can see how things go," she stalled. She wasn't sure she'd want to see him if there was no future beyond being fun-seeking friends. Usually she used her spare

time between assignments to do laundry, pay bills and sleep in.

Though the thought he wanted to see her gratified her, she wasn't sure it was in her own best interests. She was getting too fond of Luis. The excitement that flared whenever he was around had escalated. She'd thought it would have faded by now, but it was stronger than ever. She listened to him when in a crowd, even if she was supposed to be conversing with someone else. She loved watching him swim, play with the boys, listen with head bent to his grandmother.

But most of all loved it when he looked at her. His gray eyes seemed to delve into her deepest thoughts. His smile caused her to smile in return. His lightest touch sent waves of longing through her. Thinking about him would cause her heart rate to increase. She stared out the window, confused as never before. This was a special time. Was it the romance of Spain? The novelty of the family she was working with?

When they arrived at *Mar Y Llevant*, she was delighted to stop worrying about the future. She'd spent enough time with her confused thoughts.

Enchanted to see the large building half on the land, she was fascinated at its construction. It stair-stepped from the sidewalk up to a section over the sea. The shore was reinforced by a retaining wall, no beach for several yards in each direction. They parked and soon were seated on the deck over the water. The breeze was pleasant and the view amazing. It felt almost as if they were on a private yacht in the middle of the sea.

They ordered the day's special. When the waiter left, Luis reached across the table to take one of Stacey's hands.

"So, what do you say?" he asked.

"About?" She knew, but she did not know her answer. Stalling, hoping the right response came she tried to analyze her feelings.

"To seeing each other once we're back in New York."

"I'd like that—when I'm home." She hoped she wouldn't continue to feel more for the man. Though when those eyes stared into hers, she could throw all caution to the wind and spend every free moment with him.

He looked satisfied and she wondered if he'd really been concerned. He must have women in New York who would love to go out with him. Saying no would have been more prudent, but beyond her tonight.

"You'll have a lot of adjustments to make when you get home," she said, teasing.

"How so?"

"Finding ways to spend more time with the boys, finding time to date. I hope your business doesn't fall flat on its face."

He shook his head, his eyes amused. "No danger of that. Though we do need to keep on top of the cutting edge of medical technology. I've hired some excellent people to work with. Can you cut back on your trips?"

"I don't know what Stephanie has scheduled. If I'm committed, it would be hard." Harder still to tell him no. She wondered if they'd grow closer back in New York or if the mystique of the vacation would fade and they'd be caught up in their former lives with no more special tie between them. She was almost afraid to find out. What if the spark died, flying across the Atlantic? She'd much prefer to hold this special holiday in her memory untarnished and perfect.

He frowned when she didn't say anything. "I know you said the summer is your busy time, but I don't want to wait until September to see you again."

Stacey shook her head. "I didn't say I have no time between assignments, just not a lot. Let's see how things work out. And if we continue to speak in Spanish, think how my fluency will blossom."

"I'm not a language teacher," he grumbled.

Stacey watched him, growing amused. She suspected Luis rarely had someone say no to him, either at work or socially. She loved being with him. She couldn't help wondering if this interest in seeing her would continue once they returned home. Caught up in his old life, he'd more than likely get caught up in work and find less and less time to seek her out. The thought disappointed her but she shook it off. Tonight they were together, exploring this new facet. She was going to enjoy every moment.

They talked about the remaining days of the vacation. The fiesta next week. His grandmother's actual birthday the day after that. Before long they'd be returning to America. She wished she could hold back time. Yet every moment spent together brought her closer to Luis.

The seafood was fresh and delicious. Stacey enjoyed it and hoped she could do it justice when reporting back to Marguerita. She told Luis of his mother's recommendation and he was surprised to learn she and his father had dined at the restaurant.

"I know a place nearby that has dancing," Luis said as the meal was winding down. "Shall we?"

"I'd love to."

The nightclub was already crowded when they arrived, but Luis found a table near the dance floor. After ordering drinks, they went to dance.

Stacey was secretly glad the first song was slow and dreamy. She felt a bit dreamy herself when he took her into his arms and held her close to his chest. She loved moving with Luis to the music. Closing her eyes, she

could imagine herself spending many evenings like this, dancing together, just the two of them. Cocooned in a world of their own, shutting the rest of the world out. They'd talk about their day. Make plans for the future. Enjoy being with each other, touching, dancing, kissing.

Not that Luis had even broached the idea of a long-term relationship, much less marriage. But still, friendship and fun could grow into intimacy and a closer relationship that might—just might—lead to something more.

She could so easily fall in love with him. He was everything anyone would cherish in a mate—good looking, successful, caring, fun to be with and sexy. And she knew at first hand he could be a devoted father. She liked watching how he and his twins related. She could see the difference from that airplane flight to yesterday at the beach.

Their evening went on until well after midnight. When they drove back to the villa, Stacey still felt dreamy. A few more evenings like this one and she'd fall so deeply in love she'd never get out. She wasn't quite daring enough to put it to the test. She needed to guard her heart. She'd pull back just a tad and take things slowly. Luis hadn't mentioned a long-term future. She knew once the novelty wore off, once routines reasserted themselves, things could change. Wishing for a future together could prove futile.

Luis stopped the car by the front door. Once again the villa was dark except for lights in the hallway. "Care for a nightcap?" he asked softly when they entered.

"Better not, those little boys get up early. I've had a wonderful time," she said.

They walked up the stairs, holding hands. Switching off the lower lights, only the one lamp in the upper hall

remained lighted, giving soft illumination to the long stretch.

They walked to her bedroom door and she turned, smiling up at him, her heart racing. "I had fun."

He rested his forehead against hers, looking deep into her eyes. "I did, too. I always do when I'm with you. Let's do it again tomorrow night."

Slowly she shook her head, rolling theirs together. "The fiesta's in a few days. That'll be fun. But in between I need to be alert with my charges. I need an early night tomorrow."

She wanted to say yes, to spend endless hours together, but she had to hold on to her emotions, even if it meant not seeing him as much as she wanted. If it was meant to be, things would work out. If not, she needed to make sure she had a way to extricate herself without heartbreak.

"I'll try to change your mind," he warned.

She laughed softly. "Do that. I look forward to seeing if it works."

He kissed her, drawing her slowly into his arms until they were pressed so tightly together not a scrap of air could get between them. His mouth was firm and tantalizing and the sensations that shot through her thrilled her. She wrapped her arms around him and kissed him back, wishing with all her heart this was the first of endless nights that ended this way.

He spun them slowly around and the world seemed to tilt. She could feel his heartbeat against her own. His mouth was warm and when his tongue touched her lips she eagerly gave way to the exploration as he deepened the kiss. She was burning up with the heat of their kiss, but wouldn't end it for anything.

Both were breathing hard when Luis slowly released

her. She relished being held by him, keeping her eyes closed, letting the emotions sweep through her. She did her best to imprint every bit of her feelings on her mind to remember forever.

"Sleep well," he said, brushing his fingertips across her lips.

She opened her eyes as she kissed them. "I shall, and you."

"Dream of me."

She smiled and entered her bedroom. His request would probably be answered without any effort on her part. It would be harder to not dream about him.

The next morning Luis was already on the terrace when Stacey and the boys arrived. The younger cousins came with them and soon the children had piled their plates and gone to their table. With no other adults present, Stacey felt she should sit with Luis. He wouldn't want to eat alone.

"Good morning," she said, placing her plate across from him and sitting down. The early morning sun was warm on her shoulders, but not yet hot.

"Up early despite your late night," he said, his look telling her without words that if they were alone he'd greet her totally differently. She felt his gaze almost like a physical touch.

"I told you those boys don't sleep in. Wait until they're teenagers. They'll hate getting up before noon." Such mundane words when she really wanted to ask him what was going on between them, where this would lead. Did he still feel the same way in daylight as he had last night? Or was it only an illusion?

He nodded. "I remember. What would you like to

do today? The beach beckons. There are other towns to visit."

"I love the beach," she said.

He laughed and Stacey caught her breath. He looked amazing, younger than before somehow. Then she realized it was the first time she'd seen him when he didn't have that air of sadness.

"The beach it is."

The next few days passed swiftly. Everyone was on the go from morning to night. From meals on the terrace to swimming in the sea, to exploration of nearby towns and historic sites, to quiet evenings in the garden. Stacey enjoyed herself tremendously—especially when Luis was present. He made every day a priority with his boys. And every evening a priority with her.

Stacey took photos and helped the boys write and draw pictures in a journal to show Hannah when they returned home. And to help them always remember this summer. They solemnly told her each evening what they'd liked best about the day for her to record. Leafing through the notebook each night, she hoped she had captured the best part of their vacation—not only for Hannah but for the boys to have in the years to come.

Her favorite time, however, was evenings in the garden. Almost every night she'd leave the crowd in the salon and slip outside to walk in the quiet garden, enjoy the serenity of the grounds. And soon after Luis would join her. They ambled through the illuminated paths, talking, laughing at things the boys had done during the day. Or rambled along the beach, sometimes wading in the water, other times sitting out of its reach and talking. He ended each evening with kisses that heated Stacey's blood. She had never been happier.

One afternoon Luis suggested they head for the vil-

lage. They bought ice cream and wandered through the old streets. The boys liked looking into the windows, asking for things that Luis would not buy for them. Not dispirited, they'd dash to the next window.

"The fiesta begins in a couple of days. I thought we'd take the boys during the day and then after dinner and fireworks take them home for bed and go back, just the two of us," he said as they finished their ice cream. "The festivities last well into the night."

"They'll want to swim the next morning. They and the cousins asked at lunch if they can do that. Otherwise, whatever you want." She found it novel to be consulted on plans. Normally she was told what the parents' plans were and she and her charges would adjust accordingly. She'd love to have a part in the boys' lives. They had changed a lot in the time they'd been in Spain.

"Then let's plan on you taking them to the beach while I catch up with the office at the internet café. Once done, I'll join you."

She smiled at him in a teasing manner. "Wow, you've been away from the computer for days. I thought you were cured."

"Smarty," he said, reaching out to touch the tip of her nose. "I have been without any updates in days. Time I at least find out what's going on and if I still have a company."

She laughed. "As if it could fold in such a short time. I thought you had competent employees."

"I do. Doesn't mean I don't want to know what's going on."

They turned and headed back toward the car, going along one of the busiest streets in the village. A sporting goods store caught Luis's eye.

"Hey, how about we get some snorkeling equipment for the kids?"

"If you get enough for everyone. I bet the kids will love to each have their own. No squabbles that way."

The next morning Isabella was the only adult at the breakfast table when Stacey came out with the children. They quickly piled food on their plates and went to their table. Stacey served herself and joined Luis's sister.

"You have known my brother for a long time?" Isabelle had arrived last of the family and had missed some of the earlier conversations.

"No, he hired me for this trip. Short notice, but I speak Spanish so I got the job."

Isabella complimented Stacey on her Spanish, asking her when she'd become so proficient. "Have you lived in Spain?"

"No, this is my first visit. At first Spanish was something to learn, but I've been able to use it on trips to Mexico and Central America. I know some of the words are different from pure Spanish, but it gave me a start."

"Tell me some of the places you've been to," she invited.

Stacey enjoyed sharing some of her experiences in remote seaside resorts, busy cosmopolitan cities, and other well-known destinations.

"It sounds like such an exciting life," Isabella said.

"I love it. Children entertain me to no end. They have a way of saying startling things, some funny, some insightful, some mean. And then I want to know why."

"I have a routine job. I like it, but wish I could travel more. Still, I wish to have a family someday and all that travel would make it hard, don't you think?"

Stacey smiled and shrugged. "It could certainly make

things more difficult. But if it's meant to be, love will find a way."

"Well, I wish love would hurry up for me!" Isabelle said.

Stacey gathered the children when breakfast was over and took them to the beach, with the large string bag that held all the snorkeling gear. The servants had already set up the beach umbrellas and the chairs, not that she'd be using them for long. She liked being in the water with the children, close at hand in case of an emergency. And for the sheer enjoyment of the sea.

The snorkeling equipment proved to be a hit with everyone and soon all the children were exploring what the sea floor held. It was shallow enough so when they found something they could stand to shout to the others.

Despite knowing Luis would be gone all morning, she scanned the beach from time to time to see if he'd changed his mind about joining them.

Midmorning Theresa, Anna and Isabella joined them. All the children were happy to see them and begged them to come into the water so they could show off their new-found skill and share masks to let the others see the amazing clarity underneath the water.

Anna plunged right in and when she reached Stacey she told her, "You go sit down for a while. We'll play with them."

"Okay, thanks. We've been racing and exploring, and keeping an eye on all of them when they go in different directions is challenging." Stacey headed for shore and one of the lounge chairs beneath the umbrella.

"Stacey, where are you going?" Pablo asked, swimming over to her.

"I'm going to sit on one of the chairs for a while. Want to come?"

"Will you tell me a story?"

"Sure."

He paddled beside her until they reached the beach and then walked with her to the lounge chairs. She pulled one more into the shade before sitting on it. Pablo scrambled up beside her. His skin was cool and wet. She brushed his wet hair off his face. He was a precious child.

"Tell me the story of the caves," he said.

She'd made up a story the night after their visit to the caves about the people who had lived in them and drawn on the walls. Delighted he wanted to hear the stories again, she began.

When she'd finished that story, Pablo asked for another. Just then Luis stepped into view. Stacey felt her heart skip a beat. Smiling, she wished she'd been able to comb her hair or something. Instead, her nose was white with sunscreen and her hair probably looked like a soggy rat's nest.

"I finished early," he said.

"So I see."

"Hi, Daddy, Stacey's telling me stories," Pablo said.

"Are they good stories?"

"Yes. She doesn't have to read them like Hannah does."

"Very good." He waved to those in the water who called to him, and pulled one of the other chairs closer, sharing the shade of the umbrella.

"While I was in the village I learned of a short ship cruise this afternoon I thought we could go on. It's a two-hour cruise along the coast. I thought you'd enjoy seeing Spain from the sea."

"Me?"

"You, me and the boys."

"I don't have to go," she said, thinking maybe he should go with just his sons.

"Yes, you do," he said with no hesitation.

Luis sat for a few minutes, then took Pablo and went to join the others in the water. Stacey elected to sit on shore and watch. That way she could focus on Luis to her heart's content and no one would be the wiser. He looked perfect, tossing children into the air so they could splash down in the water. Their laughter rang out. He seemed to be enjoying himself as well. She knew she'd never get enough of watching him, so this was a special treat.

It was hard to pry the children away when time to rinse off the sea water and dress for lunch.

The midday meal proved to be full of chatter as all the children tried to tell Abuela Maria, again sitting at their table, about the snorkeling. She laughed and nodded approvingly at Luis.

After lunch, Luis, Stacey and the twins took off for the cruise. They parked near the marina and walked down the long dock to the large yacht moored at the end.

"I expected sails," Stacey said, admiring the ship.

"It's big," Juan said.

They joined several other passengers on the wide deck and soon the boat cast off the mooring lines and slowly pulled away from the dock. It headed north toward France as it held steady about a mile off the shore. With the breeze blowing, it was pleasant on the water. There was plenty of room near the rail to stand and study the coastline. The boys soon grew bored and wanted to see how the captain "drove" the boat.

"I'll check with him to see if it's okay for you to observe. But you are not to touch a thing," Luis said.

Stacey stayed by the rail and soon Luis joined her, covering one of her hands on the rail.

"They're set?" she asked.

"He's happy to have them. Even let them sit on one of the high seats so they can see ahead as well as around. They had a thousand questions."

"I hope his patience holds out," Stacey said, conscious of the tingling sensation sparkling through her with Luis's touch. "I love this. Did you ever think of buying a boat?"

"Never. I know very little about sailing and have even less time to learn."

"There's lots of nice spots off Long Island or Connecticut where you could moor a boat and sail."

"Maybe when the boys are older."

Stacey asked what he wanted for the boys when they were older and then what he saw as his future when they grew up and moved out on their own.

Luis grew pensive. "I always thought Melissa and I would tour the world or something and then welcome grandchildren at some stage."

"You'll have the grandchildren. And there's still time for trips, it's not as if you're in your nineties yet," she gently teased, wondering for the first time where she would be if she lived to be ninety. She didn't want to be without family to celebrate birthdays and holidays with. The yearning for a family of her own grew stronger.

"How about you?" Luis asked.

"I've never thought that far ahead. Life each day brings a lot of rewards." She didn't want to confess that the life she thought she'd forever love was beginning to pale. That other situations held more appeal. She had done what she'd set out to do when she'd begun Vacation Nannies. Did she wish to continue traveling as much, al-

ways a nomad? It had sounded the perfect life five years ago. And she'd seen all the continents except Antarctica. When would she reach enough?

Was it time to change plans? Recognize new dreams?

"I'll have to give the future some thought when I return home," she said.

The afternoon was delightful. Stacey enjoyed every moment and was happy when Pablo sought her out to tell her all about how he'd helped with the captain of the boat. He and Juan had received little sailor caps to wear, which they did proudly.

"Dinner on our own?" Luis suggested when they docked. "I told grandmother it would be unlikely we'd be home for dinner. Sometimes it's so noisy I feel like I'm in a crowded restaurant."

"Everyone's happy to see each other and wants to share their news."

"I know, but I like the quieter meals—with you." He smiled into her eyes and she felt another frisson of anticipation. He was flirting. But did it mean anything serious?

"I like that, too," she admitted.

After a family dinner in the village, the four of them returned to the villa in time for the boys to go to bed, and Luis helped. He rarely put them to bed in New York. Normally they were asleep by the time he returned home. Here it seemed like a normal part of the family routine. He tucked them in, kissing each in turn. How long before they'd be too old to tuck in, to hug and kiss? He'd like this night-time ritual to continue as long as possible.

He also liked listening to Stacey tell them stories. Their rapt expressions as they followed her every word touched his heart. These children were entrusted to him

to raise without a mother's influence. It was up to him. The thought was awesome. Scary on one level, challenging on another. And more a pleasure than a duty.

He spent as much time watching Stacey as he did the boys. Her stories were exciting and adventuresome, yet totally suited to the boys' level of understanding. No big, fancy words, no convoluted plots. He wondered if she told stories to older children. If not, those charges had missed something special.

She was special.

He drew a deep breath. He'd had his shot at love, and it had ended sadly. He dared not risk his heart again.

Yet how could he say goodbye at the end of their vacation?

After bidding the boys goodnight, he asked Stacey for a walk in the garden.

"For a little while," she said. They turned out the bedroom lights and headed downstairs together.

The garden's many paths were bathed in low-lying lights. The fragrance of the night blooming jasmine filled the air. They meandered along, enjoying the quiet night with the scattering of stars overhead. Finally Luis gestured to one of the benches almost hidden in a shrubbery alcove.

"Today was perfect. They boys are thriving here," Stacey said as she sat down.

"Not only thriving, but better behaved as well. You remember that first day? I had threatened them with dire consequences if they didn't behave. Sometimes I'd cut short an outing because of their unruly behavior. But I've never see it when they're with you."

"Firm guidelines help," she murmured.

I agree. But it's more than that. They have other chil-

dren to play with here, other relatives who take an interested in them." He looked at her. "You're good for them."

Her eyes sparkled in the dim light. Her hair looked like a golden halo around her face. He could look at Stacey all day long.

"I'm glad you think so. That's part of the service, you know, make friends, ensure the children have the best vacation they can. I'm going to miss them."

"They're going to miss you." He fell silent, gazing around at the garden that was his grandmother's joy. She'd lived in this house all her married life. Never traveled very much. Yet she had a serenity and contentment he envied.

Would it make sense to raise his sons nearby? Abuela Maria wouldn't live forever. He wanted them to know her and to always remember her. Sebastian and Teresa and the other cousins were within driving distance. What did he have in New York? A company, a few business associates.

And Stacey.

Closing down the feelings that clamored to break forth, he rose abruptly.

She looked up in surprise.

"I have to go in," he said. Knowing he was acting like an idiot, nevertheless he needed distance from Stacey. He could forget his own vow to stay safe by not becoming entangled with another woman. He could forget his own name when around her.

"I'll stay here for a little while longer," she said, looking at the low row of flowers lining that portion of the pathway.

"See you in the morning." He couldn't wait until daylight, when he'd not be swayed by romantic settings. The fiesta would be demanding and lively. The boys would

love it. And the time between now and then would give him a chance to think things through clearly.

He hurried toward the house. Changing his mind, he went to the garage and got his car. A drive would chase away futile thoughts. He had his children, his business, his life had been going just the way he wanted it. Now it all threatened to implode.

CHAPTER EIGHT

THE entire household was in high spirits at breakfast the next morning. The children who had been to fiesta before could hardly sit still, and their joyful excitement was shared by the twins. Even the adults were in a hurry to get to the village.

"It'll be so much fun," Theresa told Stacey. "There's so much to see, a parade at noon, and lots of fun activities for all of the family. Even Abuela Maria attends."

"But I won't be participating in all the activities as I once did," the older woman said, but the brightness in her eyes attested to her excitement of the day.

"And tomorrow's your birthday," Jose said. "We'll have two days in a row to celebrate."

"But not a birthday party as extensive as fiesta, thank you," Maria said. "A fine day with the family is all I wish."

"Fireworks on the beach would be nice," Anna said.

"When we were younger," Theresa explained to Stacey, "we had fireworks on the beach. But that's been banned for a number of years now. Too dangerous in the hands of amateurs."

"It sounds like fun." Stacey was pleased Luis seemed his normal self this morning. After the abrupt way he had left her last night, she had been worried about how

to greet him. But when she'd said good morning, he'd smiled at her and replied. She was not sure how things stood, but for today she'd push aside her own confusion and doubts and make sure the twins had the best fiesta ever.

As soon as breakfast was over, everyone prepared to head for town. Because of parking difficulties, Maria arranged for her chauffeur to take everyone down in shifts and return for them when they called.

It took three trips for everyone to get to town, but since the round trip took less than ten minutes, everyone gathered together in a short time.

Juan and Pablo clung to Stacey's hands, staring around them in awe. There were colorful banners flying in the breeze, booths and concession stands lining the main thoroughfare, which had been closed to vehicular traffic for the event. Everything under the sun was for sale, it seemed. Toys, jewelry, food. Further along near the beach were the games and carnival rides for children. The crowds swelling the streets couldn't all be from Alta Parisa. People had come from all over to celebrate fiesta.

"They've never been to anything like this," Luis said softly over her shoulder.

She looked back at him. He was close enough to feel his breath skim across her cheek. He looked down at her, then looked away. Turning slightly, he asked his cousin Sebastian where he wanted to start.

For the rest of the morning until it was time for the parade, Luis kept his distance from Stacey. At first she wasn't sure, but after a while she knew that any time she came near him, he managed to put several people between them. Once she'd realized that, she began to pay more attention to the boys and ignore Luis. If he didn't want to share the experience with them, that was his de-

cision. She was going to have a great day and make sure the twins did as well.

When the parade started, the entire family was lined up on one curb, the children leaning over to peer down the street as the parade began. Small camp stools had been brought for Abuela Maria and Sophia. Their excitement was evident even after all the years they must have seen this parade.

First was the relic of the patron saint of the village, carried by several young men of the town. Cheers arose as it was carried by. Next a contingency of officials. Anna leaned over to Stacey. "The mayor. Obviously the highlight of his term of office," she murmured as the man beamed and waved to everyone.

Then a local band marched by, playing a lively song. A group of equestrians, clowns, the local fire engine, spritzing water left and right to the delight of the children. Then a convertible with people sitting up on the back, tossing candy left and right. Children scrambled onto the street to snatch as much candy as they could. More entries followed. Some were simple, others elaborate, but all were fun. For a small village, it was a grand parade.

"I'm hungry," Juan said as the end of the parade passed by—a police car that sounded its klaxon every few feet.

"Me, too," Pablo said.

"Me, too," Stacey said. "Let's check with your father and see what his plans are,"

Anna pointed towards the water.

"There're open tents down at the end of the block for lunch. We can grab something from any of the booths and sit in the shade while we eat."

"Sounds like a great idea." Stacey took the boys,

bought them food and then joined Anna and Theresa and the others at the tables they had secured in the open tent. The space was huge and crowded with those enjoying the fiesta.

She glanced around as she got the boys settled, but didn't see Luis. Or Sebastian or Jose either.

"The men probably went to get the wine," Theresa said, settling in. Her plate was piled high with paella. Stacey had bought hamburgers for the boys.

"It's nice to sit for a minute," Anna said.

"Can we go on the carnival rides after lunch?" Pedro asked his mother.

"Probably. We'll check with your father. I think we've seen most of the booths and some rides would be fun."

"Abuela Maria is going back soon. I think after the rides I'll take Alli back and we'll both take a nap. Fireworks don't start until after nine and then there's the dancing. I don't want to miss that."

Stacey listened as the cousins talked. She didn't know if the boys would be able to stay up for fireworks, but knew they'd love them if they could.

Luis and his cousins found the others in the tent and joined them, pouring wine for all the adults, teasing the younger members of the family about getting old enough to drink. He sat beside his grandmother, down the long table from his sons. And Stacey.

"Having fun?" he asked the older woman.

He began to eat as his grandmother studied him a moment. "You don't need to sit with me, Luis. Go and sit with your children."

He glanced down the table. Juan was talking up a storm and the others were laughing from time to time. From his pleased expression, Luis knew he enjoyed the

attention. Pablo sat quietly at Stacey's side, laughing with the rest.

It was Stacey who held his attention the longest. She was beautiful when she laughed. Her eyes sparkled and when she exchanged glances with Pablo, he could tell his son was thrilled to be sitting beside her. He'd be thrilled, too. But it was better to keep his distance. He'd decided that last night. This thing with Stacey was moving too fast. He wasn't even sure where it was moving. But he was not going to rush any change.

"Melissa would have adored her sons," Maria said softly. "But she isn't here and I doubt she'd want them to grow up without a mother's influence."

He glanced at her. "They have a very suitable nanny," he said.

"Maybe. But it's not quite the same," she suggested, resting her aged hand on top of his. "You should think of remarrying."

"Grandfather died over five years ago, yet you haven't remarried," he reminded her. He didn't need this. He'd decided during his drive last night to concentrate on his sons and his business, ensuring they never wanted for anything.

"Luis, don't be silly. That's different. Our children were grown long ago. Our grandchildren are grown. He was able to meet most of his great-grandchildren before he died. But you, dear grandson, are still quite young. You have most of your life ahead of you and it should be shared."

He patted her hand while he shook his head. "I was married. I loved Melissa. I still miss her. I just couldn't go through something like that again."

"What makes you think you would?"

"There are no guarantees in life," he said.

"True. But look around you. Are your cousins braver than you? Each of us could die tonight, but that doesn't mean we don't grab all of life we can today. Play what-if and suppose you live to be a hundred. What wonderful memories will you have to look back on? Who will share your reminiscences? Who will you share your children with, your grandchildren?"

"It's not as easy as you think," he said.

"Nothing worthwhile in life is. Dare to take a chance. I want you happy and your family happy. Maybe even some more grandchildren? A little girl, perhaps?"

He laughed. "I'll consider it." He flicked another glance down the table, then returned to his meal. He would consider it, just as he'd said, and refuse. Life was fine the way it was.

After lunch Maria and Sophia returned to the villa. After the children rode on the carnival rides, they were taken back to the villa, protesting all the way. Stacey put the twins down and despite their assertions they were not sleepy, they fell asleep within minutes of being put to bed.

She went to her own room to lie down to rest. Luis had stayed in town and she expected he was on the internet, keeping in touch with his office. Fiesta day in Alta Parisa didn't mean a holiday in New York.

The rest of the afternoon passed quickly. The children took a short swim in the sea, ate dinner and were ready to return to the fiesta for the fireworks. During the entire time Luis had been missing. Stacey couldn't understand why he didn't want to spend time with his sons. He was missing so much. She'd seen the change earlier, as he'd spent more time with them. Why of all days did he pick this one to be away?

Abuela Maria organized everyone's trip back to the fiesta. She arranged space in the town square, already filling up with families and courting couples wanting the best vantage point for the fireworks. Maria had several chairs brought down for her and Sophia and the other women. The children sprawled on blankets spread out on the limited space available to them. The church dominated one side of the square, the other three sides had businesses and restaurants and shops all doing a booming trade. As were the stalls and booths lining the sidewalks.

As it grew darker, Luis joined the group, sitting near Juan and Pablo. The boys were in high spirits. Stacey considered sitting with them, but when Luis arrived, she decided to give them their time together.

The first explosion caught the crowd by surprise. In no time, everyone focused on the light spectacular in the sky. The oohs and ahhs were universal and everyone enjoyed the display. Stacey noticed Pablo climbed into his father's lap and lean back to watch. Juan was too restless to sit still for long, but from time to time he leaned against Luis's shoulder as the pyrotechnics continued. Finally, in the traditional burst of many at once, the event was over.

Theresa leaned over to speak to Stacey. "I'll take your boys home with me and put them to bed. Stay and enjoy the rest of the fiesta. I'm too tired to stay. I thought a nap would help, but it didn't."

Jose and Alli came over and he reached to help fold the chairs. "Ready to go back?" he asked Theresa.

"Yes, I'm so tired. It's been a fun fiesta, but not my last, so let's get home and to bed."

Stacey debated relinquishing the boys but the plan met with Luis's approval and soon the older and younger

members of the group had left and only couples remained. Stacey suddenly felt awkward. She should have
gone back. From Luis's reaction last night, the last thing
he probably wanted was to be paired with her.

"Let's go to the café on the beach and see if we can
squeeze in," Sebastian said, hugging Anna close to him.
"There's dancing."

"I'm all for that," his wife said, skipping a step. "And
no children to hamper us!"

Luis stood beside Stacey. "That okay with you?"

"Fine with me. How about you?"

"It's fiesta, a night to have fun."

She heard the unspoken warning. *One night for fun,
don't get any ideas.*

The rest of the evening was entertaining. They found a
table for two, squeezed in more chairs. When the drinks
arrived, they filled the small table, but no one cared. The
music was the best Stacey had heard and she danced the
night away. In light of the festive nature of the event,
the music was lively and fast. She regretted at one point
that there wasn't at least one slow dance. But foolish
thoughts were best ignored. Being around Luis was poi-
gnant enough.

She could spend the rest of her life with him. Only he
wasn't interested in the rest of their lives, only tonight.
She refused to let that dampen her spirits. She'd have the
best time she could, and then remember it whenever she
was feeling low.

When they decided to call it a night, Sebastian called
for the car from the villa. When it arrived a short time
later, he ushered the women into it, saying he and the others would wait for the second trip. Stacey hid her disap-
pointment with a forced smile. No chance of a goodnight
kiss—unless she hung around, waiting for Luis to return

to the villa. She had too much pride for that. Wistfully she remembered their shared kisses. She'd been living in a fantasy world. And as their time left in Spain grew shorter, she knew Luis had decided to rein in any time with her lest she get the wrong idea. Once home, it was back to their individual lives.

She only had a few more days on this assignment. She'd never expected to be included in so many family activities, almost as if she were one of them. Which she definitely was not. Her next assignment would be waiting. She'd have no time to dwell on might-have-beens.

But she wished she could. Wished Luis would open his heart to the possibility of a future together.

Once at the villa, she hurried upstairs to check on the boys and then headed for her room. A quick shower and she climbed into bed, the French doors open to the breeze and the faint sound of the celebrations still going on in the village drifting in.

She closed her eyes but sleep didn't come. Instead, she considered her feelings for Luis. She had never felt so close to any other client. To any other man. He awakened longings she'd never expected. And gave her a boatload of ideas that warred with what she'd thought she wanted for her future.

Giving up on sleep, she let herself daydream that Luis loved her. The fantasy of becoming a family with him and the boys wouldn't go away. Maybe before they left Luis would tell her again that he wanted to see her when they returned to New York. She'd make time to see him and maybe if he suggested marriage, she'd say yes. What a joyful time they could have raising raise Juan and Pablo and maybe a few children of their own. She was visualizing them happily living in a huge apartment in New York when she heard him in the room next door.

She held her breath.

Had the men stayed longer in the village? Or had a nightcap downstairs? It didn't matter. The fantasy image vanished. Reality crashed down. Sighing, she rolled on her side and tried to go to sleep.

The hours slowly dragged by. Finally Stacey pushed back the sheets and rose. Slipping silently out onto the balcony, she went to the railing and looked out over the garden. The soft path lights gave a warm glow. The shrubs and flowers were all various shades of gray except where immediately by a light. She leaned over and drew in a breath. The sweetness of the flowers filled the night air.

"Couldn't sleep?" Luis asked.

She spun around. He stood in the doorway to his room. Stacey's first impulse was to flee back to hers. She wore only her light cotton nightgown. Still, in the darkness she was practically invisible.

"Too much excitement at the fiesta, I guess. The dancing was fun." Being with you was fun.

He walked to the railing, staying about ten feet away. "The twins loved it. I guess they've only seen fireworks from a distance. We'll have to go to the display on the river on Independence Day."

"They'd love that." She looked back to the garden, conscious of his nearness, his distance.

"Tomorrow is Abuela's birthday," he said. "I know she's delighted as many of her family as could gather have done so. We'll be heading for home afterward, one family at a time. As much as I resisted coming, I'm glad we did. She's loved it and the twins have gotten to know other relatives."

"That part's been nice for them. I hope you plan fu-

ture visits so they can keep in touch. Think how much they and the other children will change in a year."

"Life can change in a heartbeat, I know," he said.

Stacey knew he was thinking of his wife.

"I know you miss her," she said softly.

"I can't go through something like that again. Ever. I refuse to be a hostage to fate."

"So it's better to shut yourself off from the possibility of happiness?" she asked. Was that the reason he'd grown distant? Was he coming to care for her and refusing to let himself go in case something happened to her?

"I'm content, it's enough," Luis said.

"What of the boys?"

"They have Hannah. She's all the mother they've known."

Stacey wanted to argue with him, tell him not everyone died in childbirth—it was extremely rare these days. But he wouldn't listen. He'd closed himself off. She didn't have it in her to change his mind.

Sadly she realized love wasn't enough. Not if it was one-sided. Instead of her love bringing her joy, it brought pain. She wished he could believe he could find love again, and have it last until he was quite old. His grandparents had had a long happy marriage from what she'd heard this visit. His own parents seemed happy enough in their marriage. He wasn't the first man to lose a wife, but he could live another fifty or sixty years—did he have to live it alone?

"I wish you love one day," she said. "All the joy and happiness it can bring."

He didn't respond. A moment later, Stacey walked back to her room and closed the French doors. She might not get back to sleep, but she didn't want to hear Luis,

didn't want to feel this hopeless yearning to be held by him, kissed, loved.

She was twenty-nine years old and had never even had a steady boyfriend she might have married. She couldn't believe she was in love with a man who refused to even consider marriage. How ironic was that?

The birthday was almost as festive as the fiesta had been. Breakfast was joyful with all the family gathered, wishing Abuela Maria happy birthday, presenting her with presents and hugs and kisses. She protested that at her age she didn't need any gifts, but seemed as excited as a girl opening each one, exclaiming to the giver how perfect the gift was. Stacey had framed a photograph she'd taken of the boys with Luis on the beach. Maria gave her a wide smile. "Perfect to remember this summer," she said.

That brought the conversation to photographs and it was soon decided to get as many as could be taken in the next days to commemorate the occasion and given to Maria. Sophia volunteered to put them in a keepsake album.

Luis's mother joined Stacey when all the presents had been opened. "What a thoughtful gift to give. I know Maria will cherish it. And as a result, she'll have lots of photos of her birthday to look at in the future."

"I'm happy she liked it."

Marguerite gestured her aside. "I hope we see more of you when we all return home."

"Thank you, but unless Luis needs a vacation nanny again in the future, it's unlikely." Stacey was proud that her voice didn't wobble when she said his name. It was all she could do to refrain from looking at him.

"We'll see then." She gave her a pat on the shoulder and moved on to talk with Anna.

The day passed as others had. Children flocked to the beach. Abuela Maria and Sophia joined them, sitting in the shade of the umbrella, walking along the water's edge from time to time, encouraging the children in their swimming and diving. Games were played. Laughter filled the air. Stacey stopped at one point and watched the Aldivista family and all the fun they were having. She hoped these children and parents realized how lucky they were.

Dinner was more formal, with several of Maria's friends invited, including Mario Sabata and his daughter. Stacey was included even though she protested she should not be. Then wished she'd stuck to her stance when she had to watch Luis play attentive host to Mario's daughter. She slipped out to her room as soon as the first guest left.

They had two more days and then would return to New York. Checking on the boys, she tucked the sheet over Juan. He was restless even in sleep. Would he always be a high-energy boy? She gently brushed the hair from Pablo's face. He was growing more confident every day. Being with other children helped him become more adventuresome. He was not relying on Juan as much, which Stacey saw as a good thing. She wondered if this vacation would change how they interacted with other children at school. She hoped her sweet little boy would enjoy school.

Only he wasn't her sweet little boy, though he held a special place in her heart. She leaned over and kissed his cheek. She was going to miss the twins so much. More than any other children she'd watched.

Sighing softly, she leaned over again and kissed first one then the other on their baby cheeks and left.

She'd miss these two boys almost as much as she was going to miss their father!

Time flew by. Departure day dawned in pouring rain—as if the heavens were weeping in sadness of the departure, Stacey thought whimsically as she finished packing the boys' clothes. Her own suitcase stood by her bedroom door. She was wearing the suit she'd flown in before, feeling the distance already begin from the fabulous vacation to the business at hand. In less than twenty-four hours she be back in her small apartment, her visit to Spain another memory to add to her collection.

"Do we have to go?" Pablo said, sitting on his bed, kicking his heels against the side.

"Maybe your father will bring you back next summer," Stacey said in Spanish. The boys had picked up a lot of the language. She hoped they would be encouraged to continue learning. So much easier when young. "When you get home, you can tell Hannah all about your visit, your cousins, aunts and uncles, grandparents. Showing her your journal will make the visit seem longer."

Juan bounced in, holding two toys. "Can I take these?"

"No, leave them here for your next visit," Stacey said. Snapping shut the fasteners, she upended the suitcase and set it by the door. "All done except for our totes. Where are the things you are taking on the plane?"

"I want to take these toys," Juan said stubbornly.

Stacey smiled and shook her head. "Not going to happen. Find your things and let's get moving. Your dad wants us downstairs at nine." Checking her watch, she felt a pang as the minutes drew closer to their time of departure. She wanted to stop time. She'd so enjoyed

this visit. And in only moments it would become just a memory.

One she'd never forget.

She had fallen love. She almost ached with sadness. She hoped Luis would never suspect. At least she could console herself with him thinking she was the best nanny he'd ever hired.

They still had the flight home. A few more hours together. Then she'd really feel differently. She hoped Savannah was home. She wanted to talk to someone about her feelings, and what if anything she could do to cope until the pain of parting faded.

The boys were as reluctant to leave Spain as they had been to leave New York three weeks earlier. Alli and Paloma and Pedro promised to write and call. Within limits, the parents said, hugging everyone. Soon Luis had them in the rental car, driving to their first airport on the journey back. At Madrid, Stacey entertained the boys while Luis made a call to New York, verifying Hannah had returned and was expecting them.

The flight across the Atlantic was easier than the one going to Spain. The boys, tired out, soon fell asleep. Pablo and Juan had both sat with Stacey once they could move about the cabin, leaving Luis's companion seat empty. He made use of the space to review files and work on his laptop. Stacey watched him as he worked, feeling her love for him blossom. His concentration was total. She wished she had the right to reach over and smooth those frown lines from his forehead, tease him into a good mood. Sit beside him and talk to him while the children slept.

But he was oblivious to her presence. Sighing gently, she reclined her seat and closed her eyes. She was tired herself and felt let down. Maybe a nap would help.

Luis stared at the laptop, unaware of what he was looking at. He could feel Stacey watching him. He wanted
to turn and see her smile, watch as her blue eyes lit up.
He only had a few hours to go and the temptation to forget the vows he'd made to himself would vanish and he
could concentrate on getting back to normal. Whatever
that would be in the future.

He'd known her such a short time. He could forget her
as quickly. He hoped. Once back in the routine of their
lives, things would settle down. It was simply a holiday infatuation. He glanced over. She was asleep. He
leaned back and closed his own eyes, not to sleep but to
remember. He could see her that first day in his office,
all pink and pretty. He now knew pink was her favorite
color, she wore it a lot. And it was perfect for her with
her light hair and blue eyes, bringing a faint pink tone
to her skin. Opening his eyes, he looked at her. She had
more tanned skin now than when they'd left New York—
from all the hours at the beach. She'd generously shared
her time with not only the twins but their young cousins
as well.

Funny how she'd fit in with his family in a way
Melissa never had. Mainly due to her ability to speak
Spanish. How quickly the boys had picked up enough to
understand most of what was said to them. He'd have to
find a way to continue that. Maybe next summer he could
find time to visit his grandmother again. If Sebastian and
Jose and their families could coordinate the same time,
Juan and Pablo would see their cousins again.

Would Stacey be available then? He'd see about booking her for a few weeks next summer.

He studied her while she slept. It wasn't often she
was in such repose. He was going to miss her. For the
boys' sake. He wondered if there was a way to fit her

into their lives. He could take more vacations, but unless they flew, Hannah would be the one accompanying them. A trip the Caribbean would ensure Stacey would be the nanny on the trip. Maybe in the fall he could take some time and take the boys snorkeling in the Virgin Islands or Bermuda.

He frowned. He was not going to use subterfuge just to see her. If they wanted to meet outside work, he'd call her up and take her to dinner or something. Maybe invite her to the Independence Day celebrations with the boys. That would work.

She shifted positions and he looked away, not wanting to be caught staring. As soon as she settled again, he looked back.

The plane continued its flight, bring New York closer by the minute. Luis wished time could be suspended for just a short while but before he knew it, the cabin attendants were preparing for landing.

CHAPTER NINE

Stacey awoke when she felt the change in cabin pressure. They twins were still asleep. She glanced across the aisle and met Luis's eyes. Smiling self-consciously, she shifted in her seat and tried to shake away the lingering sleep. Only a few more minutes and they'd land. Her assignment was finished.

She woke the boys and had Juan go and sit next to his father for the landing.

"We'll be on the ground in a few minutes," she said to Pablo.

"I wish we were still in Spain. I liked the sea."

"Me, too. Maybe Hannah will take you to the shore this summer. Or your father." She'd bet the twins would have more of a chance with Hannah.

"You could take us," Pablo said hopefully, looking at her.

"Oh, honey, I can't. I'll be working. Remember I'm just the vacation nanny. Soon you'll be back with Hannah and your regular life."

"Where will you be? Can't you come with us?" His eyes were wide as he stared in dismay.

"I don't know where I'll be. I go different places all the time. I'm not home a lot, especially in the summer. But maybe we'll meet up again someday."

The prospect of traveling all summer now seemed like a dreaded assignment. She'd love to take the twins to the beach. Especially if Luis came. She would want to know what they were doing until school started again. When Juan's loose tooth came out and how far behind him Pablo's baby teeth would be lost. There was so much she wanted to know about them. And most likely never would.

The minutes seemed to fly as fast as the plane. They continued descending. She looked out the window. "Look, Pablo, we can see land now."

He looked out the window and then back at her. "When will you come visit us? Can't you stay with us?"

"Honey, Hannah's waiting at home for you. She'll be so glad to see you."

"But I want you," he said plaintively.

"I'll tell you what. If your daddy takes another vacation to Spain, maybe he'll call and ask for me to go with you. Then I'd see you again."

Pablo leaned over her and called to his father. "Daddy, can we go back to Spain so Stacey can go with us?"

Luis looked at Stacey. "Maybe in a few months. We just finished our visit there."

"But Stacey won't go home with us."

Juan leaned over. "Why not?"

Luis turned to him. "Stacey only went with us to Spain because Hannah couldn't go. Hannah's your regular nanny. She'll be home when we get there and so happy to see you."

Juan pouted and sat back, folding his arms across his chest. "I want Stacey. She speaks Spanish, Hannah doesn't."

Luis hid a smile. Three weeks ago the boys hadn't

even known there was another language out there, now this was the reason he wanted Stacey.

He looked across the aisle. It sounded as good as any. He wanted Stacey, too.

The plane glided in for a landing. The passengers began to gather belongings in anticipation of reaching the gate. Stacey had the boys' tote loaded, her own ready to go. Once off the plane her duties would end. Better to separate at the airport than stretch out the goodbyes any longer than she needed to. She'd never found it so hard to bid her employer farewell. She hoped she could hold onto her emotions—just a little longer.

Being in first class, they were among the first to disembark from the plane. Luis took the boys' tote and offered to take Stacey's, but she kept hers.

"I'll just say goodbye here," she said when they'd cleared customs and were in the main concourse. "I need the ladies' anyway."

"We can wait," he said. The boys looked at her in dismay.

"No need. Thanks for a great assignment." She would keep her voice upbeat and neutral. The threat of tears hovered but she refused to let a single one fall.

"Bye," she said, hugging Pablo and kissing his cheek. She repeated the action with Juan. Standing up, she smiled at Luis, her heart breaking. "Think of Vacation Nannies if you take a trip abroad again."

"Stacey, wait."

For a split second she thought he'd change his mind about taking a chance. Might even go as far as want to see her again.

"I hate to just say goodbye here," he said after a moment.

She studied his dear face, memorizing every feature.

The sandy hair didn't seem so out of place now for a daring Spaniard. His grey eyes would forever be imprinted on her mind. A thousand images flashed through her mind, each one bringing heartbreak. She felt tears well.

"Here or at the sidewalk by your flat, it doesn't matter. Best of everything in the future to you." She turned and ducked into the nearby ladies' room. Once she was in a stall, she sagged. Hanging her tote on the hook, she shut the door and reached for tissue paper to blot her eyes as the tears began to fall. Trying to muffle her crying, she hoped no one would hear her.

She hadn't wanted to say good bye at all, she'd wanted him to say she needed to be a part of their lives. To insist he had to see her again—and not for business. To see if the attraction they felt would grow into something lasting.

Not that she needed to see if love would last. She knew it would be a long time before she got over Luis Aldivista.

But he hadn't said anything. Not even goodbye.

Luis stood in the concourse as people jostled by. He couldn't believe Stacey had just left like that.

"Can we go, Daddy?" Juan asked.

"We'll wait another minute for Stacey," he said. He had wanted to broach the possibility of them seeing each other on a casual basis.

He felt a tug from Pablo. But he couldn't move from the spot. He had to wait for Stacey. There was so much left unsaid.

"Daddy, I need to go to the bathroom," Pablo said, tugging on Luis's arm again.

Great, just what he needed. The porter stood nearby with the cart with their bags that had been cleared

through customs. Luis turned and told the man they'd be right back.

"Okay, the men's room is over here," he said, trying to hurry the boys along.

By the time the twins had used the facilities and washed their hands, at least five minutes or more had passed. Luis hustled them out and looked toward the ladies. Had Stacey come out already? He scanned the area, but there were too many people to find one petite woman with blonde hair and beautiful blue eyes.

Maybe she'd be at the curb. He should have insisted they share a cab. He nodded to the patiently waiting porter and they hurried from the terminal.

Ten minutes later Luis gave up in defeat. Stacey had not been at the curb where taxies queued up to take arriving passengers to their destinations.

He hadn't thought ahead. He knew the assignment was considered over when they landed. But somehow he'd thought—what? That she'd go home with them? That the connection they'd made meant more than just a routine job?

Yet *he* was guilty of putting the brakes on any further relationship.

His mother's farewell words echoed as he hailed a cab. *Don't let this one go.*

"Let's go home, boys," he said to his children, forgetting for a moment where they were and speaking in Spanish.

They replied in kind. Stacey was right, they needed to know that side of their heritage. And the language. He'd have to see about getting a tutor for them.

What else had Stacey been right about?

Spending more time with the boys. Seeing them for who they were, not mirror images of their mother.

Learning how precious their childhood was and wanting to enjoy every moment.

And awakening feeling he'd never expected to have again.

Stacey settled back in the cab and gazed out the window, not consciously noting anything she saw, her mind back in the terminal with Luis and the boys. Her luck had held. She'd found a waiting cab immediately upon stepping out of the terminal. She didn't know what had happened to Luis and the boys, but suspected a bathroom stop there as well. She blinked her eyes again and tried recover some semblance of normalcy. So she had fallen for her boss, no big deal. She'd fall out of love as fast. Another assignment, another country and she'd forget Luis and his silvery eyes. She'd hardly remember his laughter or the kindness to his grandmother. A month tops and she'd have trouble remembering his name, the way his eyes crinkled when he smiled. The touch of his mouth against hers.

And pigs could fly.

Sighing she silently urged the cab faster. The sooner she was home the sooner she could begin forgetting the most unforgettable man she'd ever met.

The apartment was empty when she arrived. She took her cases into her bedroom and dumped them on the bed. She'd unpack soon. First she needed to know where Savannah was. Calling the office, she had that answer—her sister was backpacking in the Sierra Nevada Mountains of California and wasn't due home for another two weeks.

"How was the assignment?" Stephanie asked.

"Good." She couldn't speak much about it for fear she'd begin crying again.

"What, no recommendation we open an office in Spain?"

"Not this time."

"Well, good. I can't imagine that. How long do you want between assignments? I have two more starting next week. I've confirmed Bethany for one, but am having trouble finding anyone else. We're going to have to get more qualified nannies or start turning down jobs."

"I don't want to do that if we can help it. I can take the one you're having trouble with—what is it?"

"Sounds okay—teen watching in Cancún, Mexico."

"On the beach?" Stacey asked. "Spanish required?"

"Right for the beach part. But they are staying at a luxury resort that caters to Americans, so I expect everyone there speaks English. Your charges are daughters of an attaché at the Mexican consulate here. He wants down time but is worried about the girls without a chaperone. Two weeks."

"Ages of the girls?"

"Twelve and fourteen, and they attend a Catholic school here in New York. When I met them, the entire family came in to see our operation and asked me as many questions as I asked them. They seemed very well behaved."

"Which can be deceiving. I'll swing by later and get the info. Sign me on."

"They leave Sunday night on a flight out of JFK. I'll have all the details here when you show up."

Two girls instead of two darling little twin boys. The Mexican sun-kissed beaches instead of the sands by the Med. And no sexy father who had changed from aloof and distant to become involved with his boys' life and stepped out of grief enough to kiss her and make her dream of a future that could never be.

* * *

Two weeks later Stacey hugged her charges goodbye and went to hail a cab. The assignment had been a dream. The parents had had their own plans, so Stacey and the girls had been on their own the entire trip. And both Bianca and Bella had been wonderfully funny girls. Stacey had needed their laughter and fun to ease the transition from Luis and his boys and the fantasy dreams she'd had about becoming a family.

She'd miss the two girls, but no more than after any other assignment. Not like with Juan and Pablo. She wondered what they were doing. How had Hannah liked their journal? Did they still speak Spanish with Luis or was that fading as the days went by? Had he switched his working hours to give more attention to his sons?

Did he ever think of her?

When she reached home her plans were simple—eat and get to bed. Glancing at the answering-machine once she walked in, she noticed it was blinking. The office was closed on Sundays, so she didn't even consider calling Stephanie for her next assignment. Time enough for that in the morning. Right now all she wanted to do was sleep.

Surprised to find Savannah not at the apartment, she checked the calendar. Hadn't Stephanie said the hiking assignment would be over by now? Maybe she'd be home in the morning. Or maybe the assignment had been extended. They usually didn't do that, but if the nanny wasn't already committed elsewhere, an extension would be allowed.

Her answering-machine blinked incessantly. Ignoring it, Stacey took a quick shower and changed into pajamas. She'd have soup for dinner. On her way to the kitchen, she pushed the Play button on the machine and heard

Stephanie's voice. "Call me when you get in. We have a problem."

The next message—also from Stephanie. "Call me right away, even before your shower." Oops. Stacey looked at the clock. It was barely six in the evening.

"Are you home yet?" Stephanie sounded a bit annoyed.

"Stacey, the schedule shows you should be home by now. Please call right away."

Stacey grew concerned with the increasing frustration in Stephanie's voice. Granted, their flight from Mexico had been delayed, but what could the problem be? If it was Savannah, Stephanie would have called her employer to contact her immediately. Still, it had to be something major—Stephanie never left messages like this.

Stacey dialed Stephanie's home number.

"Stacey?" she answered immediately.

"Yes, what's up?"

"What happened on your assignment in Spain? Luis Aldivista is refusing to pay."

"What?"

"He said he needs to speak to you personally. When I told him you were already on another assignment, he asked where. You know I don't give out that information. So then he says if we want payment, you'd better contact him."

"I can't believe that. What's wrong with him?"

"I don't know but he's called every day since you left. Says he needs to talk to you and he won't be put off. I don't know what to do. You'll be off again and I want to make sure you deal with this first."

"Of course I will. Did he say why he's refusing to pay?"

"No. Just insists he has to talk to you. Honestly, I don't want him bad-mouthing the firm. One disgruntled client

could keep a half dozen from contacting us. What happened there?"

"Nothing. It was a great assignment. They boys had a lot of fun, they learned some Spanish, got to know their relatives—" She stopped. She didn't need this reminder. Images of dinner on the terrace, walks in the garden, dancing at the café near the sea flashed into her mind.

"I'll call him in the morning," she said, hoping she could clear her head so she could sleep tonight. Too many nights lately had been full of Luis and her love for him.

"You'd better, because he'll call the office at nine on the dot if last week's anything to go by," Stephanie said.

What was Luis thinking? Stacey wondered. She'd done an excellent job with his boys. Had she not, he wouldn't have waited until they returned home to tell her.

Stacey's first thought was to pick up the phone and call Luis. But she hesitated. This was business. She would treat it totally like business and call him at his office in the morning.

The hours seemed to drag by and more than once Stacey questioned her decision. She looked in the phone book and did not find Luis's name listed. That took care of that. She knew where he lived, but not his home phone. No, she would have to wait until morning.

Then she'd find out why he was withholding payment. As far as she was concerned, he had no reason in the world.

The next morning Stacey was up early. She dressed in a business suit in preparation to confront Luis, a navy suit with crisp white blouse and just a touch of red with the enameled pin at her lapel. She took her time with her make-up too. She was a professional woman in charge of

a thriving business. One aspect was to ensure satisfied customers. She'd work out whatever perceived wrong he had. If she kept her composure and didn't get angry. How dared he refuse to pay?

Arriving at his office shortly before nine, she hoped she was forestalling the call to Vacation Nannies. She didn't need Stephanie on her case.

Luis's secretary came to the reception area to greet Stacey.

"I don't have an appointment, but need to see Luis," Stacey said.

"I'm glad you're finally here. He's been like a bear with a sore paw ever since he got back from Spain," the secretary said as she escorted Stacey back to Luis's office.

"We had a lovely trip. What's wrong?" she asked.

"I don't know, only that I've placed a call to Vacation Nannies every day since he got back."

"He knows summer's our busy time. I told him we were booked almost non-stop until September. He could have dealt with Stephanie."

"Still, the squeaky wheel gets the attention and I guess he figured that's what it'd take to get your attention," she said. Despite her grouchy boss, her eyes twinkled.

"Trust me, not paying our invoice got my attention," Stacey said dryly. She could feel anticipation rise. She was going to see him again! She hoped she could focus on business and not behave like a star-struck teenager.

Much as she'd cried herself to sleep the last couple of weeks, she had not stopped thinking about Luis and hoping a way to keep in touch would be found. Disputing a bill, however, wasn't the way she wanted to do that. She had envisioned more along the lines of bumping into each other at a deli and eating lunch together. Or find-

ing he liked some of the museums she did and took the boys one day when she was there.

She took a breath when his secretary knocked on the office door and pushed it open.

"Stacey Williams is here to see you," she said to the man behind the desk.

Luis looked up as Stacey entered the office. He put down his pen and leaned back in the chair, surprised at how he felt at seeing her again. It was as if the world had righted itself somehow.

She looked glowing. She still had her tan. Her hair was pulled back, but surely looked blonder than before. He could feel the attraction skyrocket.

She wore a stylish navy blue suit, short skirt, long legs. He'd have preferred her hair loose, but she wouldn't know that. The blue eyes that stared at him were most familiar. A delightful sight to see, even if they held traces of anger and annoyance. His heart pounded.

Stacey glanced over her shoulder until the door was shut, then looked back at Luis. He tried to judge whether she was as glad to see him as he was her. But her expression gave nothing away. "My office manager says you refuse to pay your bill. Is there a reason?"

He came around the desk, wanting to pull her into his arms and kiss her, tell her how much he'd missed her since they'd parted. Instead, he walked towards her warily aware of the anger in her eyes.

"It was a ploy," he said, stopping in front of the desk, leaning against it slightly. He tilted his head to study her. She looked fantastic. Just as he'd seen her every night in his dreams. Well, not quite. Some of those dreams had been almost erotic in nature.

"For?" she asked.

"For seeing you again."

She blinked and raised both eyebrows. "You could have just called and asked to see me."

"I did. Stephanie said you were out of town."

"I was."

"So quickly? We just got home Friday and Monday you were gone?"

She nodded. "I told you we get booked up in summer. I have another assignment starting tomorrow."

"Cancel it."

"Are you crazy?"

"I think so."

She stared at him in surprise. "What did you say?

"I haven't stopped thinking about you for a single minute since you left us at JFK. I've never done that before, so maybe I'm slipping into insanity. There could be a cure, however."

She shook her head. "You *are* crazy."

Luis took courage from the slight flush on her cheeks. Maybe she wasn't as cool and collected as she looked.

"I've missed you, Stacey."

She nodded. "How are the boys?"

"Missing you, too."

"I miss them."

"And?"

"And you, too."

He stepped away from the desk and crossed the short distance until he was almost touching her. Tentatively leaning over, his gazed locked with hers, he brushed his lips across hers. When he heard her soft sigh, he gave in to his initial impulse and pulled her into his arms, kissing her like he'd never stop. She felt right in his arms. He held her closely, enjoying the feeling of her body pressed to his, the satisfaction of her arms holding him tightly. She wasn't indifferent by any means.

Finally he broke the kiss, pulling her over so he could lean against the desk, still holding her.

"Wow," she said, looking up at him, her eyes sparkling again. For a moment Luis felt the happiest man in the world. But things needed to be said. Nothing was guaranteed, now or in the future.

"I love you," he blurted out.

She widened her eyes in surprise. "What? I thought you weren't ever going to fall in love again."

"That's what you have to say to me? No 'I love you' back?" This wasn't going the way he'd hoped. He hadn't misread the signs, had he? She had to love him back.

Slowly she began to smile. "Tell me more about this love of yours."

"I loved my first wife and I was devastated when she died. I don't wish that kind of pain on anyone. And it changed me. Who expects to be widowed at twenty-six? If she could die so young, what was to prevent another woman dying young? I didn't want to feel that pain of loss ever again."

"So you decided to close yourself off from the world and focus on your company?" she said, already knowing that.

"Something like that."

"Even neglecting your twins," she said.

"They reminded me so much of her."

"They look like you."

He nodded. "This trip I really saw them for who they are—Pablo and Juan, individuals in their own right. Looking exactly like each other, yet when their personalities shine through they're totally different. They have some of her and some of me. And some of you."

"Some of me?" Stacey looked startled.

"You made a huge difference in their lives in that short

vacation. Pablo's changed the most. But Juan has as well. So that's part of you that makes up who they are. But the biggest change is in me."

She smiled again. "Do tell."

"I would die if anything happened to you. I fought against caring, but how can I resist when you're everything that I'd ever want in life? I gave myself a dozen reasons for not falling in love. But somehow my heart refused to listen. So I'm confessing how I feel and hope and pray you feel the same. I want you to marry me, grow old with me, have kids with me. Love me."

"Wow, when you change your mind, you go all the way."

"I love you, Stacey. I love everything about you, from the way you stand up to me, the way you make life a glorious adventure, the way you look at my sons, the way you laughed at my grandmother's jokes. I can't list all the ways I love you. But mostly I love when you look at me—as if I'm the only person in the world. I want you to look like that from now until the end of our days. If it's a short time or long, I want every minute. I love you. Please, will you marry me? Marry us?"

Stacey stared at him for a long moment, seeing the absolute sincerity in his eyes.

"I love you, too." She was touched by the way he closed his eyes for a second, as if in thanksgiving. "Wow, marriage and kids and the whole works?"

"Yes. Will you?" he said, his eyes looking deep into hers. Where he saw all the love in her for him.

"Yes, yes, yes!" She hugged him when he stood and spun her around and around.

She laughed and kissed him. He lowered her to her feet and kissed her back.

Moments later Luis led the way to the sofa along one

wall of his office. "I promise I'll devote my attention to you and the boys and not spend so much time at the office. We'll have a wonderful life together. And when you want to travel, we'll head wherever you want."

"Oh, my job. Luis, I have jobs lined up throughout the summer." What could she do? She was scheduled for almost the entire summer. "Stephanie will just have to work miracles. We already talked about hiring more nannies. I can screen them. There's no way I'm going to take off for weeks at a time now!"

"I understand if there are obligations you can't get out of. But I stand ready to help make sure you stay home however I can. Wait until we tell the boys. They've complained every day about missing you. They will be thrilled," Luis said, linking their hands, his thumb gently rubbing the back of her hand.

"I've missed them. Let's go tell them together."

"How about we get married in the fall?"

She nodded, smiling. "Oh, I have to find Savannah and tell her. She'll be so surprised. She wasn't home when I got back from Spain, so doesn't even know how I felt. She's going to flip when she finds out we're getting married."

"In a happy way, I hope," he said.

"Yes, in a very happy way. She'll love you and the boys."

"You know I have the twins. How would you feel about another baby or two?"

She smiled again, her heart soaring. He wanted a baby with her. And, truthfully, much as she adored the twins, she'd love to have a baby with Luis. Maybe more than one. "I love the idea of more babies. Don't forget I love children. The more the merrier!"

"So this summer we'll go to the shore, maybe drive

to New England. Get to know each other even better."
He kissed her again.

"Oh, Luis, is this real?'

"I sure hope so. I love you, Stacey, and I always will."

"I love you, too. And I always will. We really are
going to get married!"

"Yes. And I think my grandmother will be most
pleased. She likes you a lot. Even my mother told me
before we left not to let you go."

"Yet you did. You said nothing about seeing each other
after that night before the fiesta."

"The foolish actions of a man scared to death. I doubt
I'll ever take a day together for granted. But being with
you outweighs the possibility of loss."

"I love you. And I love the boys."

"They love you. They've asked after you every day
since we landed."

"What about Hannah?" she asked.

"Until we're sure how this is going to work with your
work and mine, I'd like her to stay on. She's been with
the boys since they were born."

"That works for me. And if we have a baby or two
ourselves, who better to help with them than another
woman with childcare experience? I would hate to have
her lose her place in your family because of me."

"You're right. She is part of our family. Let's go tell
them all. Then I'm taking you shopping for a ring!" Luis
said, wanting the entire world to know Stacey was his.
Taking a risk like this didn't seem so daring when it was
Stacey. She was worth everything.

* * * * *

ROMANCE

Roccanti's Marriage Revenge	Lynne Graham
The Devil and Miss Jones	Kate Walker
Sheikh Without a Heart	Sandra Marton
Savas's Wildcat	Anne McAllister
The Argentinian's Solace	Susan Stephens
A Wicked Persuasion	Catherine George
Girl on a Diamond Pedestal	Maisey Yates
The Theotokis Inheritance	Susanne James
The Good, the Bad and the Wild	Heidi Rice
The Ex Who Hired Her	Kate Hardy
A Bride for the Island Prince	Rebecca Winters
Pregnant with the Prince's Child	Raye Morgan
The Nanny and the Boss's Twins	Barbara McMahon
Once a Cowboy...	Patricia Thayer
Mr Right at the Wrong Time	Nikki Logan
When Chocolate Is Not Enough...	Nina Harrington
Sydney Harbour Hospital: Luca's Bad Girl	Amy Andrews
Falling for the Sheikh She Shouldn't	Fiona McArthur

HISTORICAL

Untamed Rogue, Scandalous Mistress	Bronwyn Scott
Honourable Doctor, Improper Arrangement	Mary Nichols
The Earl Plays With Fire	Isabelle Goddard
His Border Bride	Blythe Gifford

MEDICAL

Dr Cinderella's Midnight Fling	Kate Hardy
Brought Together by Baby	Margaret McDonagh
The Firebrand Who Unlocked His Heart	Anne Fraser
One Month to Become a Mum	Louisa George

Mills & Boon® Large Print

March 2012

ROMANCE

The Power of Vasilii	Penny Jordan
The Real Rio D'Aquila	Sandra Marton
A Shameful Consequence	Carol Marinelli
A Dangerous Infatuation	Chantelle Shaw
How a Cowboy Stole Her Heart	Donna Alward
Tall, Dark, Texas Ranger	Patricia Thayer
The Boy is Back in Town	Nina Harrington
Just An Ordinary Girl?	Jackie Braun

HISTORICAL

The Lady Gambles	Carole Mortimer
Lady Rosabella's Ruse	Ann Lethbridge
The Viscount's Scandalous Return	Anne Ashley
The Viking's Touch	Joanna Fulford

MEDICAL

Cort Mason – Dr Delectable	Carol Marinelli
Survival Guide to Dating Your Boss	Fiona McArthur
Return of the Maverick	Sue MacKay
It Started with a Pregnancy	Scarlet Wilson
Italian Doctor, No Strings Attached	Kate Hardy
Miracle Times Two	Josie Metcalfe

Mills & Boon® Hardback
April 2012

ROMANCE

A Deal at the Altar	Lynne Graham
Return of the Moralis Wife	Jacqueline Baird
Gianni's Pride	Kim Lawrence
Undone by his Touch	Annie West
The Legend of de Marco	Abby Green
Stepping out of the Shadows	Robyn Donald
Deserving of his Diamonds?	Melanie Milburne
Girl Behind the Scandalous Reputation	Michelle Conder
Redemption of a Hollywood Starlet	Kimberly Lang
Cracking the Dating Code	Kelly Hunter
The Cattle King's Bride	Margaret Way
Inherited: Expectant Cinderella	Myrna Mackenzie
The Man Who Saw Her Beauty	Michelle Douglas
The Last Real Cowboy	Donna Alward
New York's Finest Rebel	Trish Wylie
The Fiancée Fiasco	Jackie Braun
Sydney Harbour Hospital: Tom's Redemption	Fiona Lowe
Summer With A French Surgeon	Margaret Barker

HISTORICAL

Dangerous Lord, Innocent Governess	Christine Merrill
Captured for the Captain's Pleasure	Ann Lethbridge
Brushed by Scandal	Gail Whitiker
Lord Libertine	Gail Ranstrom

MEDICAL

Georgie's Big Greek Wedding?	Emily Forbes
The Nurse's Not-So-Secret Scandal	Wendy S. Marcus
Dr Right All Along	Joanna Neil
Doctor on Her Doorstep	Annie Claydon

0312 GEN STD HB

Mills & Boon® Large Print

April 2012

ROMANCE

Jewel in His Crown	Lynne Graham
The Man Every Woman Wants	Miranda Lee
Once a Ferrara Wife...	Sarah Morgan
Not Fit for a King?	Jane Porter
Snowbound with Her Hero	Rebecca Winters
Flirting with Italian	Liz Fielding
Firefighter Under the Mistletoe	Melissa McClone
The Tycoon Who Healed Her Heart	Melissa James

HISTORICAL

The Lady Forfeits	Carole Mortimer
Valiant Soldier, Beautiful Enemy	Diane Gaston
Winning the War Hero's Heart	Mary Nichols
Hostage Bride	Anne Herries

MEDICAL

Breaking Her No-Dates Rule	Emily Forbes
Waking Up With Dr Off-Limits	Amy Andrews
Tempted by Dr Daisy	Caroline Anderson
The Fiancée He Can't Forget	Caroline Anderson
A Cotswold Christmas Bride	Joanna Neil
All She Wants For Christmas	Annie Claydon

GEN STD LP

D1486624